THE JAGUAR KING

L. E. Zimmerman

BAD CREATIVE BOOKS

Did you know an African Leopard can carry prey twice its body weight up vertical tree trunks? That's over four hundred (400) pounds for fully grown males. Beastly.

This book is a work of fiction. Names, characters, places and incidents are products of the author's imagination or are used fictitiously. Any resemblance to actual events or locales or persons, living or dead, is entirely coincidental.

ISBN 9798617112667

Cover art by Gestvlt

OTHER BADCREATIVE BOOKS

Bewitching Amelia
Banking On Love

The Simplest Way To Learn French 2017

The Simplest Way To Learn Spanish 2017

Managing Complications In Anesthesia And Critical Care

Table Of Contents

Prologue

The Jaguar King

Long ago, a secret society of humans existed which sought to gather and pool together their respective resources, knowledge and wealth from their different nations, to form a new world order that would have a deeper hand in the state of all affairs around the globe. The society held a great power which others did not: the ability to shapeshift into leopards. They were known as the Jan Damis, all of which comprised of various people of different countries. The Jan Damis were renowned and feared for such a vaunted ability that lent them great power and mercurial stealth. At the head of the society, was a revered shaman of sorts that had lived for centuries, and yet did not age. This shaman was known as the leopard king, the man who brought the source of the Jan Damis's power to the society.

The Jan Damis founded their headquarters in a stone temple in the remote islands of Porto da Cunha. Over time, the Jan Damis grew in power and were shortly after in the thick of many world events. From the Revolutionary War, to the isolationism in feudal Japan, to the trades between Britain and India, and even aiding Napoleon in conquering Italy, no event around the world transpired without the Jan Damis present. The only traces of their influence were oft the recounting of people swearing they saw a person turn into a leopard and disappear.

Throughout time, the Jan Damis also began hunting their most ferocious enemy: the race of the wyverns. While the draconic rulers of the sky were indeed powerful, the Jan Damis had numbers, resources, information, and their deadly ability to sniff out wyvern lairs and lay slaughter to them. Over time, the numbers of the wyverns were greatly trimmed, until less than one hundred of them remained. The last of the mighty wyverns then banded together and went into hiding far from the reaches of civilization. Despite living in constant fear of the leopard shifters, the wyvern took small solace in knowing they could survive for the time being.

In addition to the nigh-extinct wyverns, the race of humans had equally come to see the Jan Damis as a growing threat, for they had limited knowledge and understanding of what the Jan Damis did, or their intentions. Banding together, they plotted a strategy to hunt the Jan Damis down in numbers and seal their powers away. An agreement was soon signed by the leader of the human faction, named Sir Ricard Vel and an elderly wyvern, Illixus, and the newly-formed alliance would come to be known as the Dracosapiens. Once established, their first step was to find a magical counter to the Jan Damis's shapeshifting powers. An answer was found after a couple years, deep in the jungles of Peru within a stone temple that wasn't unlike the Jan Damis's own: a sealing talisman called the Oro Luna.

During the expedition, a handful of the explorers found rows of etchings on the temple's walls that displayed what looked to be leopards turning into humans and back. One of them depicted the imagery of a leopard with a glowing crown above its head, and another had the same leopard battling another leopard with some sort of clothing around its neck. Beneath them lay an altar with a glowing stone orb upon it. A thrilling discovery it was for the Dracosapiens expedition team; for right there, in the lush jungles of the Peruvian temple, was believed to have been the source of the Jan Damis's powers. Once obtained, the Oro Luna was taken back to the Dracosapiens' headquarters based in Iceland.

As the expedition party returned to their home base, Sir Ricard and Illixus greeted the others. "Well met, friends. Tell us, did you find anything?" Sir Ricard said to the lead explorer with a worried face. The lead explorer nodded as he took out the fabled talisman from his pack. Sir Ricard took the artefact in his hands and inspected it. A simple interlocking pattern of squares was carved into the talisman, followed by a faint glow of crimson light. Gasping, Illixus huffed in a deep, gravelly voice, "Is this it?" The lead explorer nodded and replied, "Yes, Master Illixus. This is the legendary Oro Luna, the counter to the Jan Damis's ability. The temple revealed drawn etchings of men turning into leopards and back, as well as scripts telling of a king of the leopard shapeshifters, and a leopard fighting him. We don't know what the leopard part was about but there was a direct inscription for the Oro Luna on what it does, and its purpose. This is indeed what we have sought."

Sir Ricard turned to Illixus, gave a knowing look, then said, "With this, we can bring down the Jan Damis. It's time to move to phase two of our plan: let us begin gathering our resources and lead small raids on the Jan Damis. We'll draw them out of their hiding places and hunt them down. Our priority is to take them captive for interrogation, get them to betray their own. If their resistance proves too difficult, kill them. They've been running amok long enough, and it is up to the Dracosapiens Alliance to end this madness."

"Not to mention, they've slain an egregious amount of my kin! They will answer in their captivity or with their blood!" Illixus huffed, anger rising in his voice. Sir Ricard patted the mighty elder wyvern on his cobalt-colored scaly skin, and said to him with a softer tone, "It's terrible what they've done to your kin, friend. We'll end this reign of madness." With that, the Dracosapiens scouting party gathered and headed for the main hall to discuss tactics and plans.

The offensive began in the summer of 1820 as the Dracosapiens executed their first three successful operations. The first strike grabbed a politician all too comfortably seated within the council of the Duchy of Braganza. The councilman was part of the Jan Damis, for he had tried to shift into his leopard form upon seizure. The Dracosapiens' s scouting team managed to subdue and successfully seal his powers with the Oro Luna present. Upon arrival back at their headquarters with the councilman hostage, multiple experiments were conducted with the talisman placed near the Jan Damis member.

After a series of tests, the Dracosapiens learned the talisman would glow a brighter crimson shade in the presence of a leopard shapeshifter, turn an eerie yellow when sealing their power, and glow green briefly when it sealed a shifter. It didn't take much to make the captured Jan Damis reveal the location of others. Sir Ricard and Illixus were both very pleased and sighed a breath of small relief, stoking the flame of hope which the Dracosapiens carried towards stopping the Jan Damis.

The second operation took place in the fall of the same year. This time, the location was in Antarctica, as the scout team had found a small encampment of sorts not too far from the frosted shores. A group of Jan Damis were leading their own expedition: a search for possible places to gather resources and even set up another base. The operation was thrown the to the wind when the scouting team arrived. Unlike the first operation, this time the Jan Damis group put up a fight where several lost their lives from getting their powers sealed away. A few did remain however, and were taken captive back to the Dracosapiens headquarters.

Their interrogation led to very potent information, including names and ranks of the Jan Damis, and a hint as to the location of their own headquarters. Gaining traction against the leopard shapeshifters, Sir Ricard and Illixus began plans for a third operation. By now, the Jan Damis were much more aware of the situation of things, and so the Dracosapiens resorted to quietly laying low for a few years, before making the next move.

In the winter of 1823, the scouting team made their way for a secluded base in Seychelles, which the Jan Damis captives had said held a key figure in their ranks. After ambushing and sealing the Jan Damis's powers off, a total of one thousand, nine hundred and fifty-two captives were taken, making it the Dracosapiens's greatest campaign yet. Once in Iceland, the members gave full disclosure about the headquarters of the Jan Damis, rumoured to be the location of the leopard king. The Dracosapiens Alliance threw a raucous party that night, in celebration of their victorious efforts. What came to follow however was less than joyful: the Jan Damis had now fully turned their attention on to the Dracosapiens.

What followed were four decades of fighting between the groups, each trying to take the other down. The Jan Damis had grown wise to the tactics of the Dracosapiens, and the ensuing results led to deterrence and espionage between the two factions. When all seemed hopeless in terms of getting to the headquarters of the secret society, a scout discovered a secret route that the Jan Damis had been using to get to their temple in Porto da Cunha. A now aging Sir Ricard met with a less aged Illixus, and formulated what would be the final operation, which would be to storm the Jan Damis's headquarters and seal the leopard king.

In the spring of 1868, after leaking a false message declaring the Dracosapiens arrival within a week or so by sea, the scouts made their way by air via the secret route to Porto da Cunha, with the aid of the wyverns. The scouts couldn't have had them any more fooled, as the dark night sky provided the cover they needed, to make their way to the tiny island. Upon landing, the scouting team stealthily made their way towards the headquarters. Surely enough, their intel proved correct, as they happened upon a stone temple of sorts with sculpted leopard statues outside of it. The scout teams all formed up and after a moment of respite, began their final operation.

The inside of the temple had various rooms, some which kept untold amounts of money from various countries, some kept items and artefacts of all sorts, spanning a diverse range of time and locales. Others had tables for what presumably looked like meeting rooms, and others yet had books and scrolls aplenty. Leading the operation as they made their way to the main hall, was none other than Sir Ricard Vel himself. In there, a feast was in order, and the sounds of the Jan Damis wolfing down fine food and drink filled the air. Sir Ricard pulled out the stone and immediately began sealing all their powers while the Jan Damis remained oblivious. Sensing something wrong, a man in ceremonial robes and garb stood and said, "Something's not right. There's something, or someone here." At the end of the sentence, the ambush of scouts lined along the high balcony, immediately responded with a hail of bullets into the crowd. The Jan Damis were caught unaware and suffered greatly for it, as they were slain nearly all to the man. The man in robes fled as Sir Ricard bellowed, "There's the leopard king! We must stop him!"

The king made his way through a passageway that led to a room with peculiar artwork of leopards and stonework. In hot pursuit behind him was Sir Ricard. Once cornered in the room with his back to the wall, the great shaman of the Jan Damis watched as Sir Ricard armed himself with the Oro Luna.

"At last, great leopard king! I have you cornered and unable to escape," Sir Ricard spoke with grim finality, vengeance rising in his tone. "I'm sure you're familiar with this stone." With that, Sir Ricard took the fated talisman out as it began to turn yellow. The leopard king felt a great tug from within his body, feeling a heavy disconnect from the source of his shapeshifting ability; his power was being sealed. What followed surprised Sir Ricard, as the leopard king's body began to dissipate in a glow of yellow light. Looking to the Dracosapiens leader, the leopard king said with a weakened voice, "The source of my power is now gone...I too will be sealed from the stone. I've far lived past my natural lifetime, and it was only my station as the leopard king that kept me alive. However, there will come a time when the world will learn of the existence of the leopard shapeshifters again. By that, they will know of me and I will swear to make my return to the living world." The yellow light flashed and when it dimmed, the leopard king was gone.

Back at the Dracosapiens headquarters, Sir Ricard brought the crown of the now-sealed leopard king to Illixus. Smiling, he said, "It has been done. We currently have other scout teams going around the world to ensure we've taken down the rest of the Jan Damis." Illixus nodded, then sighed in relief, one that he seemed to have held for nearly a century.

"Very good. At last, the rest of my kin can come out from hiding and live the rest of their days in peace," Illixus stated. Looking to the sky, he continued on, "This has been a taxing campaign, doubly so on you, old friend. You've spent much of your short human life in honouring your commitment to the alliance." Sir Ricard grinned from behind a white, neatly trimmed beard and replied, "It was well worth it. The Jan Damis would've ended up being their own world power if left unchecked, and not one born of a nation. What do you suggest we do with the Oro Luna?" Illixus looked out into the distance and said, "I know of a mountain where I could hide it. It's better if the world does not know of what transpired here. We'll keep what information and records we do have in the books here, as well as what the scouts recover from the Jan Damis headquarters. Obviously, this will fade into the annals of history and into legend over time, but better that than openly reveal to others who may rise to do what the leopard king did."

"Some explorers went back to the temple to try to better study and understand the inscriptions as one" said the lead archaeologist, "What are you hoping to find in this temple?" Illixus asked. Taking a piece of paper and charcoal, the man lay various parchments across the pictures and writings and made several rough tracings with what he found. Looking to his assistant, he replied, "Perhaps there's more to this story than what the original team found decades back. The story of the leopard king and the leopard. People don't leave inscriptions like that without some sort of cause or reason."

The tracings were analysed and written down by the lead explorer named Edis DuMont. He had kept a series of journals over the years, trying to understand more about the leopard shapeshifters. He found in his research that a tribe of Incans once partook of a ritual that involved drinking leopard blood after enchanting it and killing it. The resultant effect being the ability to change into leopards. Edis was obsessed with the wealth of knowledge he learned, and would later pass his research on to his children when he grew into late age, just before his passage in 1881.

In 1890, Sir Ricard Vel passed away and was lain to rest by Illixus himself. What remained of the wyvern population continued to live in secrecy, but had the freedom to choose where they went. The Dracosapiens had been mostly disbanded two years after the successes off the final operation, but kept in contact with one another. Throughout the next century, only very few of the children of the old alliance members would know of what happened. Time went on and the threat of the Jan Damis was gone. All was right in the world again for another century or so. Until the summer of 1990...

Chapter 1: Enter Sam Cruz

Across the chilly mountain range in Keystone, Colorado, the sun was unchecked in the gorgeous blue sky, shining gallantly across the grassy expanse of open land. In the distance, the snow-capped mountains stood mightily in their serene majesty, adding a lovely backdrop to the expanse. A young man named Sam Cruz ran a hand through his shaggy brown hair, took in a deep breath and proudly exhaled the crisp air, his dark eyes drinking in the magnificent sight before him. Another young man next to him, with blue eyes, short blond hair and light skin said to him, "Hey Sam, you excited for your first year of college here?" Sam nodded and replied, "Oh man, I sure am! This is certainly a change from Florida, that's for sure. The sun here isn't as warm, but my olive skin will still hopefully maintain its tan, yeah?" Sam's friend shook his head and chuckled before saying, "Well, get used to the cold here at the very least."

"Fred Dolwick, I'm proud to call you my childhood friend. Look at us, we're here. It's almost surreal. Never in my life would I have thought I'd leave Florida, but here we are, standing in Keystone, about to embark on our first year of college here." Fred looked to Sam, clapped a hand on his shoulder and replied, "You're such a homebody, I don't think you would've even left Jacksonville if I didn't goad you with your parents." Sam laughed and replied, "Certainly that. Thank you for pushing me to take this jump. Now then, shall we go explore the downtown?"

The two headed back to Sam's yellow jeep and went on their way to the next stop of their trip. Sometime later, the two parked outside of a lodge-themed restaurant and went inside. The restaurant had pillars and beams made of logs, smoothed down and well-built into the frame holding up the metal awning. A large moose head was posted up on top of the awning, only adding to the rustic allure of the eatery. Inside, the scent of a warm fire burning wood in the large fireplace across the way, mixed with the savoury scents of hot food being cooked up. Smoked meats, frothing beers, fries hissing from the pans started wafting into the nostrils of both Fred and Sam. The two took a table near a window that sat nicely near the fireplace and scooted into the oaken table.

"Wow, great recommendation, Fred," Sam said, taking his jacket off and looking over the menu." Fred did the same and responded, "I heard great things from the Sigma Pi guys I've been talking to. Figured we'd give it a shot. Speaking of, are you ready for the Sigma Pi initiation ritual coming up?" Sam motioned to one of the waitresses before saying to Fred, "I feel ready enough. I'm not sure what we're doing, but making a trek up Mount Elbert for the weekend is already exciting enough." A waitress with red hair and green eyes came up to their table, smiled and said, "Hello! Welcome to SRV Steakhouse! My name is Sara, may I take your order?" Fred eagerly replied, "I'll take a rare bear steak and some sweet tea." Sam looked to her and said, "What do you recommend here?"

"Well, the elk burgers are terrific here. The hot wings are also popular, as well as the buffalo steak," she replied. Sam thought for a moment, then said, "Sorry for the wait, first time here. I'm new: I'll try the elk burger and get a coffee on the side. Medium cooked." Sara nodded, then said, "Oh, newcomer? Well then, welcome to Keystone! Hope you enjoy it here," Sara said with a smile and a wink before taking their menus and leaving. Fred looked to Sam with a grin and teased, "Oh wow, I think she fancies you a bit."

"Dude shut up! I simply said I was new here!" Sam replied, starting to feel his ears grow hot. Fred laughed and continued, "I don't know, man. She seemed rather intrigued." Sam blushed at the notion as Fred chuckled. Continuing, he said, "So, I don't know much about the initiation itself since the Sigma Pi are tight-lipped on it. But I do know hiking up Mount Elbert is going to be sweet." Sam nodded and replied, "Maybe we're going to camp up there?" Fred replied, "We could very well be doing that. Ooh! Maybe we're going to hunt an animal to eat!" Sam put his hands on the table, leaned forward as his expression grew intense.

"You really think so?!" That would be awesome!" he exclaimed, excitement taking him over. Fred added, "Oh yeah, that's what I'm hoping! A rugged hike and hunt to land our own food. I'm all for it!"

Moments later, Sara approached the table with their drinks and food, saying, "Here we are: a tea, a coffee, a bear steak and an elk burger. Hope you enjoy it! Welcome to Keystone," taking a glance at Sam again with a smile before leaving. Sam looked to a grinning Fred and said, "Shut up and just eat." Fred could only laugh.

Both plates were incredible to the young men, as Sam hungrily bit into the large burger. The spices and seasonings were all prepared to a pinnacle of preparation. They all complimented each other to deliver a delectable taste to the palette. The elk was a new taste to Sam, where the remnants of its gamey taste held, but complimented the flavor. Fred's food was not really appealing as he cut into the hunk of bear meat in front of him. A thin layer of red juice and fat seeped from the cut, as a pink and red colour showed inside the incision. The taste was something Fred had never experienced. A note of its strong flavor overtook him, one that had him eagerly tearing into more of it. Both Sam and Fred gave each other knowing looks of great delight and continued their delightful lunch.

Chapter 2: Sigma Pi Preparation

By evening, the two young men had made their way to their dorm and began packing their hiking gear. The dorms were arranged as large cabins for members to all live near campus, adding to the appeal of the location for students in their college selections. In their cabin room, there were two smaller rooms with two beds on each side. Both had a small desk and lamp to work from, as well as a main room with two couches, a coffee table, a drawer with a TV on top it, and a small kitchenette where any residents could cook. "Well Fred, this will be everything we need, I suppose," Sam said, gathering his bag. Fred slung his bag onto his desk and said, "Pretty much covers it. We head out tomorrow morning with the Sigma Pi committee: the trip should only take us a couple hours or so." Sam placed his bag on his bed post and asked, "What's so special about Mount Elbert? Why there?"
"Perhaps it being the highest mountain in Colorado? It does have the tallest elevation of 14,439 feet." Sam digested the information for a moment, then asked, "Huh. That's valid. You don't think that maybe there's some sort of myth or legend up there?" Fred shrugged his shoulders and replied, "I don't know. Maybe Bigfoot is up there? Maybe it's just because of the title of highest mountain in the state."
"That's fair," Sam replied. Fred walked over to the refrigerator and grabbed two beers, popping the top off and handing one to Sam. Both taking a seat on each couch, Sam took a sip and said, "I'm getting more and more excited for this, Fred." Fred nodded and looked out the window to admire the sun setting behind the mountains in the distance. As it did, the chill grew colder and seeped in through the half-opened windows.
"I heard a tale from the locals around here before you arrived a few months back," Fred said, turning his focus to Sam, after a moment of silence. Sam took another swig and replied, "Oh yeah? What's the story?" Fred quaffed some of his beer and said, "Apparently, this town used to be home to a few members of a group that dealt with a secret society back in the day. I'm not sure what it all entailed, but they stopped this group that had a hand with governments and the like. Deep-state level connections." Sam listened with rapt attention and replied, "Really? What happened then?" Fred continued, "They stopped the leader of the group and that was the end of it. I didn't get much in terms of in-depth details, but it makes for a good tale that some of the locals are fond

of. Makes you really wonder about government conspiracies a bit more too."
Sam put his beer down on the table and replied, "Wow, that is something indeed. Any other local legends?" Fred took another glug of his drink and replied, "Aside from that, not much. Some of the people tell your usual folklore fable, like Skinwalkers or wendigos. Which I'll admit, are creepy themselves." Sam glanced out the window briefly and then replied, "Well, hopefully we don't run into any of those while we're on the hike tomorrow. Getting up and going over to the windows to close them, Sam peeked outside, just to allay his own nerves of the tales. Fred

chuckled and replied, "Don't see any wendigos, do you?" Sam closed the windows and retorted, "I don't, thankfully."
The next morning, the duo made their way up the road to arrive on campus. Pulling up to a large three-story house, the words ***SIGMA PI*** were embossed on the sill of the first floor. Stone steps led up to the door, which had a group of what Sam and Fred presumed to be Sigma Pi members. Parking and exiting the jeep, Sam and Fred were approached by a young man, a few inches taller than the two. He wore a bright red varsity jacket and had a slim figure. His facial features were sharp, only offset by a shadow of stubble. Wearing a crew cut, he came down the steps and greeted the two.
"Ah, Samuel Cruz and Frediel Dolwick! The name's Bradley Davidson, president and head of Sigma Pi. I'm glad you made it well. We've our travel group ready for your induction and initiation: would you like to follow us in your vehicle or ride in one of ours?" Bradley said, with a nasal voice. Fred and Sam shook hands with him as Fred replied, "Glad to meet you. We'll take our vehicle, appreciate your offer though." Bradley shrugged and said, "No worries, figured we'd extend the offer. I hope you guys have your hiking gear ready."
"That we do, as well as camping gear, if need be," Fred replied. Bradley smiled and motioned for the others to head to their vehicles. Turning to the two, Bradley said in what Sam perceived as an almost condescending tone, "Smart fellas, you two! I'm sure you're going to love the trip. Very well, follow my car out of here and we'll make our way to Mount Elbert." Sam and Fred headed for the jeep and started it, following Bradley's car onto the road.

Chapter 3: The Awakening

The drive to Mount Elbert was one of serene sights and cheerful calm. Across the canvas of grass, a collective of vibrant yellow and royal violet flowers sat upon the verdant sheen of grass, all meshing into a blur as the convoy of vehicles continued their way. Clouds rolled lazily in the sky, as the sun was breaking above the ridge. The air was chilly and crisp as Sam watched his breath appear before his face in a hazy huff.

"Fred, this is going to be great," Sam spoke, a smile taking over his youthful features. Fred shook his head and replied, "You're like a kid waiting to open his presents on Christmas. Hey, speaking of opening things: reach back in the cooler and grab me a breakfast burrito, will you? It'd be wise to fuel up before this long trek." Sam reached back to open the top of the dark red cooler in the backseat and swung it up. Grabbing two of the burritos they cooked earlier in the morning, Fred and Sam tore into their breakfast with anticipation.

A flavourful mixture of scrambled eggs with melted cheddar cheese, onions and peppers fired up their taste buds and expedited their consumption. Feeling much more prepared, Sam reached back to the cooler to pull two water bottles out and put them in the cupholders. Both immediately began hydrating, as the occasional sight of civilization would pass in the background off to the sides of the road.

"Have to say Sam, you're a hell of cook," Fred said, breaking up the silence in the jeep. Sam grinned and replied, "Gotta teach you how to do it sometime."

"Tell you what, you teach me to cook, I'll teach you how to talk with women better. Sound good?"

"Oh, come on! Not this again." Sam looked at Fred with a scowl as Fred laughed and replied, "You've been like this since we were younger, dude. Ten years later, you're still a shy buck." Sam focused his gaze to the mountains, cracked a small smile which Fred didn't let go unnoticed and replied, "Okay, deal. Until then, focus on the road and let's get to Mount Elbert."

After a couple of hours, the convoy reached a parking lot that sat at the base of the largest mountain Sam had ever seen. Everyone got out of their vehicles to stretch and grab their belongings, Bradley approached the two, flourished an outstretched arm to the mountain and said, "Welcome to Mount Elbert, tallest mountain in Colorado! Here, we'll begin our hike. It's going to be roughly seven hours or so, depending on how fast or slow we all move."

"I see," said Fred. "Well then, let's all get a good stretch and then move out." Everyone in the group gathered around, roughly twelve in all as Bradley brought them in for what was to be the preliminary hiking speech.

"Sigma Pi," Bradley began with a deep breath and resounding tone, "We have arrived at the hallowed induction ground for our two new pledge brothers, Sam Cruz and Fred Dolwick, for they've passed the first and second phase of entry to our sacred fraternity. Upon the top of this summit, lies the grounds for their final test into the brotherhood. We will travel as a group and march with pride up this arduous trek, arm in arm and once again conquer the hike!" The fraternity listened with rapt attention. Despite hearing the speech before, the fraternity members still grew excited whenever they heard it. Bradley raised a fist in the air and continued, "The order has entered many with this test, so shall we continue with our new initiates. Let us begin the trek up the mountain!" The Sigma Pi, as well as Sam and Fred cheered loudly, and all turned to the mountain trail to begin the hike.

The hike was a rather pleasant one, many of the Sigma Pi members all talked with Fred, Sam and one another to break up the monotony. The group traversed over a wooden bridge that crossed a small creek. The sound of flowing water beneath their feet only bolstered their spirits. Aspen trees surrounded the trail, giving off a subtle and pleasant scent as the party continued onwards.

The occasional break was taken to drink and munch on provisional foods like trail mix, smoked jerky and fruits, or to give their feet respite. As they day went on, the temperature started to drop with the ascending heights. The wind began to blow harder, less trees were around to shelter the fraternity from its onslaught, and the elevation change was beginning to make the young men breathe harder from the thinning air.

It had been four hours in when Sam and Fred donned their jackets, due to Bradley instructing the group to do so, warning everyone that the climb was only going to get colder yet. The sun was one of the few sources of respite, beaming warmly onto the group. Peering up the trail, the path precariously led into a white and gray landscape that canvased across the top of the mountain. Sam felt an inescapable feeling of absolute diminutiveness, a feeling of being overshadowed by the mountain. The sight of unbowed enormity loomed above him: despite having scaled a significant amount of the mountain, more was above, more to let him know he was but a small soul in the world. The feeling wasn't intimidating to him, so much as it was one of respect. Humility. Oneness in knowing he was a microscopic part of something much greater. Sam couldn't stop himself from smiling as the group continued their ascent.

Another handful of hours later, the sun was beginning to paint its warm, glowing farewell to the day, as it began sinking for its daily rest. Ahead, the path had an end in sight. Bradley looked back to the group and yelled, "Not much farther now, boys! A few more miles and we'll be there!" Despite feeling their exhaustion, the fraternity all renewed their strength and quickened the pace to reach the end. Half an hour later, the fraternity reached a point where the trail ended at an incline, with nothing but rocks at the top. Sam looked to Fred excitedly, catching his breath, huffing, "We made it, buddy!"

A half hour later, the fraternity all were recouping, drinking from a bottle of vodka, eating their food, and talking of the success of the hike. They were all gathered around a lantern in the middle, and grew silent as Bradley stood up, ready to make another speech. Clearing his throat, he took a dramatic posture and said, "Now, we've all made it to the top and achieved the hike. As you know, that part of the induction is probably the hardest. Now, we will move on to the final part of the ceremony." The fraternity all focused their eyes on Bradley as he pointed to a part of the ceremony and continued, "There, is a spot that is rumoured to house a great spirit of power. We will hold a séance there to finish the induction." The others cheered as Sam and Fred exchanged puzzled glances.

The fraternity got up, as did Sam and Fred, leading them to the spot. All that was shown at the marked area was some sort of bone protruding out of the summit. "X marks the spot" said Bradley, as he walked up to the calcified Excalibur and gave it a quick, open palmed tap, before wincing in pain for a brief second. Sam felt a sudden weight press on him, getting the gut feeling that something wasn't right. Bradley said to him, "Come, Sam and Fred! Let us begin!" The fraternity looked at the two with rapt attention, their faces solemn and unnerving. Sam felt his stomach drop, his worry with the situation rising. Anxiety began to set in as he uneasily said, "Bradley, I don't think this is a good idea."

"What's wrong, Sam?" he asked, unfazed. Sam replied, "I was always raised to respect the dead. To not mess with the paranormal." The fraternity started to push them closer to the spot and dread washed over Sam, the pressure only adding to his worry. Fred looked to Bradley and said, "Hey, he's not comfortable with it. Respect his wishes with it." Bradley looked to him and replied, "This is the final test to become Sigma Pi. It's just a séance. Nothing will happen." The fraternity began chanting something in a different language neither Fred nor Sam could make out, as they were ushered to the spot. Taking a lantern, Bradley held it up and joined in the chanting. Sam started to feel dizzy as Fred looked to him and asked, "Sam, are you good?" Sam felt the air around him grow heavier, almost as if the air had taken on twice its original heft.

The chanting eventually started to fade away, and the darkness of the night seemed to encircle closer to the spot. Sam could hear a whisper in his head. He focused on it, and despite being scared, the fog around his mind only grew thicker. Soon, the entrancing whisper became multiple, a cacophony of voices, all speaking in a language he didn't understand. He felt his blood grow hot and the hairs on his arms stood on end, as the weight seemed to naturally have an epicentre from the bone. The only thing he could see clearly was Bradley's leering face, glowing in the growing darkness. All the whispers grew to chants in unearthly, low voices, voices that seemed to put Sam at ease. His head was swimming as he looked and could make out Fred's face in the darkness. He was saying something with a worried look on his face as he turned back to Bradley. The voices grew louder until they nearly overwhelmed Sam. With no warning, all of them suddenly died out, except one.

The voice said one thing to him that stirred a reverberation in his stomach.

"Por la sangria."

Sam saw Bradley slowly moving to Fred, who seemed highly distressed. He threw a punch at Bradley and caught him in the mouth as blood flew from his lip. Angered, Bassey went after Fred in retaliation. Sam felt something overwhelm him when he saw Fred receive a blow in the side: something that went beyond anger. The other Sigma Pi members now had looks of concern which seemed geared towards Fred, as Sam slogged through the weighted darkness to reach Fred, and saw Bradley throw a punch in what seemed a staggered motion. The moment his fist connected with Sam's face, a jolt he had never felt before lit his body up and sent his nerves into overdrive.

A yellow light flashed from the bone and the darkness instantly washed away. As if his body knew exactly what to do after the jolt, Sam moved back in to take another shot at Bradley. He reflexively dodged another punch and countered with his own, his left fist shooting out and catching Bradley on the chin. Bradley staggered back, then made another charge for Sam. Weaving and bobbing around a series of punches, Sam countered with a block to move inside, followed by his right knee smashing into Bradley's gut. Sam was untouchable as Bradley struggled to hit him. Time only seemed to slow for Sam, making reading Bradley's attacks much easier. Two more punches put Bradley down as he finally dropped to the ground.

His heart racing, blood pumping and senses on high, Sam looked around at the others. The fraternity was silent, while Fred, nursing a bloody nose, looked at Sam with incredulity. Sam turned back to the fraternity and shouted, "THIS IS HOW YOU INDUCT SIGMA PI MEMBERS? IS THIS HOW YOU LIKE TO DO IT? THEN WHY DOESN'T SOMEONE ELSE GET INDUCTED AGAIN THROUGH ME? COME ON!" Another flash of yellow light glowed, and didn't relent the second time around, only growing in intensity. Everyone covered their eyes, as a loud noise that sounded like roaring winds erupted from the bone. Many yellow lights exploded from the spot and swirled around the group, before shining to a blinding brilliance. The light seemed to overwhelm everyone as they all dropped to the ground and passed out.

Chapter 4: Rebirth

Awakening in the darkness, Sam felt his head swimming from the depths of unconsciousness as his senses returned. Looking around, he saw the sprawled-out forms of the fraternity and Fred, all starting to stir. Sam's head was throbbing as he looked to Fred, who weakly said to him, "Dude, are you okay?" Fred stretched his neck side to side, replying with a pained tone, "Yeah, I'll live." Looking dead into his eyes, he said, "Sam, what in the hell was that?"

"What was what?" Sam replied, unsure of what Fred was asking. Looking around at the other fraternity members, they all looked at one another, then Sam, as one said, "...what happened...what was that?" They all turned to Sam as he meekly replied, "I don't know. Bradley attacked Fred...and I fought back for my friend." The others helped both Sam and Fred to their feet as another said, "Speaking of, where is Bradley?" They all scanned the immediate area as panic began to spread amongst their numbers. Nothing but the darkness of night and the glow of a few lanterns replied. Sam said to the others, "We need to find him!"

One member said, "We stand a good chance to get lost on the way back. No one else but us is up here. Chances are, he probably went off somewhere." Taking one of the lanterns, Fred inspected the ground and saw the mild outlines of footprints walking away from the spot, before disappearing over the side.

"Hey guys, I found footprints. I don't think he was taken or anything like that. It looks like he left." One member crossed his arms and asked, "Why would he just leave? Especially at night atop the mountain." Another came up to him and replied, "Look, if he left, that's his deal. We've still got two initiates up here that just got inducted in the worst way possible." All eyes turned back to Fred and Sam; the feeling of unease returned to put Sam's nerves on edge again. One walked up to him with a grim face that after a moment, turned to a smile and said, "I'm sorry Bradley did that. He shouldn't have been so brazen with his actions. We usually only chant as you would over the bone: he never tries to step to someone like that. Well, until tonight. You both made it up here, and you gave him a solid beating for defending your friend. As vice president of the fraternity, welcome to Sigma Pi!" The young man shook both Fred and Sam's hands as a cheer erupted from the group.

The vice president had dark skin, short black curly hair, an athletic build and a notable southern tone. He said to the two, "Name's

Donte Michaels. Welcome to the brotherhood." Fred and Sam
returned the grins, and after a few minutes of congratulations from
the others, silence returned to the mountain. Sam suddenly asked,
"Hey, what is that bone, anyway?"
The group turned to the bone as Donte replied, "Good question.
Up until tonight, we never questioned it. But that weird ass light?
Something isn't good with that." Sam looked at Donte with
bursting curiosity as he asked, "Does that happen with every
induction?!" Donte shook his head and replied, "Hell nah. This is a
first, as well as a last time for that." Fred looked to Donte and said,
"Come on, let's check it out."

The fraternity made their way to the bone and inspected it. As they did, Sam felt a tug on his being to it, as if some invisible cable was reeling him in towards it. Sam held the lantern closer to see what looked like the tip of the biggest bone he had ever seen.

"Man, this looks like a dinosaur bone," he spoke, with all the Sigma Pi members looking closely at it. The curved bone ran the length of Fred's arm from ground to tip. Fred ran his hand over the smooth bone and said, "Whatever it is, it looks like it's attached to something massive. And haunted." Sam saw a red stain on the middle of it. Pointing to it, he said, "Guys, I think there's blood on here." Fred took a closer look at it, and replied, "Yep. Probably from the scuffle." Donte looked to Fred and said, "Well, I'm done scoping this thing out if you are. We'll have to make a new induction ritual after this. No way in hell I wanna see something like that ever again." The others stepped away from the morbid protrusion and made their way back to the camp.

The rest of the night passed uneventfully as drinks and food were consumed again, jest and talk were made, and toasts were had to Sam and Fred. Eventually, the Sigma Pi members made their way to bed, which Sam and Fred did as well. Climbing into their tent, Fred asked Sam, "Dude. What in the hell did you do?" Sam looked to Fred and replied, his hands held up, "I don't know! I swear, I didn't do anything!" Fred quickly shot back, "Not that! I mean against Bradley! How did you fight so well? You haven't been in a scrap ever, and yet you moved with the ease of a pro boxer!"

"I don't know. I just felt angry, and then it was like I just knew what to do. Time slowed down. My body almost moved on its own. Every blow he threw, I saw coming in half-speed and countered accordingly," Sam replied, looking at his hands. His knuckles still had the reddened marks of combat on his hands and throbbed a bit. Fred nodded for a moment, then replied, "I see. Well, whatever it was, that was awesome. I appreciate you jumping in for me." Sam grinned and said, "Fred, you're my friend. I'll gladly fight against anyone that messes with you."

"I've no doubt. And you seem to do it well. Now then, why don't we sleep and recover from the events of today? My legs and face hurt, though the face shot was from that dick, Bradley." Sam flopped down on his bedroll and sleeping bag, responding, "Yeah, I'm beat too. It's best we forget the earlier parts and just go back to campus tomorrow." An obvious feeling of unease at the events from a couple hours earlier hung over the camp, the fraternity members all digesting the supernatural occurrence that happened, as well as Bradley's disappearance. The calm night and sound of a gentle breeze flapping softly against the tents, helped lull the young men to sleep.

That night, Sam dreamt of a lush jungle in which he was moving with blinding speed, as a thrilling rush of blood took him over. His senses were acutely tuned in to something, and his dash through the green underbrush was a blur as he felt himself close in on something. Laying low, his heart pounded with ravenous need for blood, his body poised to strike. Out in the open, a boar was panting heavily, its flank bleeding from a series of gashes. The scent of something between copper and iron only drove Sam crazier as he crept upon it. The boar grunted and turned to where Sam was, but it was too late. Sam sprung forth with an impressive amount of hang time. Time seemed slowed as he looked down to the boar. The tusked swine turned to run, but Sam was quicker, as his body dove with wild fury and lethal poise, taking down and tumbling with the boar. His mouth found its neck and clamped down hard, tearing into the soft, precious jugular bloodline.

Chapter 5: Strange New Spirit

Sam woke with a jolt and shot upright in his sleeping bag. He scanned the tent, making sure he wasn't in the jungle. Looking around, he saw dawn had arrived as the soft, faint glow of sunlight poured in from the open top. Unzipping the tent, he poked his head outside to see the others eating breakfast and hydrating. Fred was there as he turned to Sam and greeted him, "Good morning. You were out like a light, how are you?"

Sam crawled out of the tent, grabbed a handful of trail mix and tore into it with ravenous hunger. He didn't recall being this hungry, except in the dream. Through a mouthful of sweet dried fruit and salted pecans, Sam replied, "I feel terrific! I would love a steak about now, though." Donte chuckled at the statement and added, "I think we all could. Sounds like we're doing a Sigma Pi steak dinner tonight then." Sam finished his mouthful of trail mix and began to break down his tent and Fred's. Fred came to help, and it wasn't long until both had their respective gear all packed again. The sun was just breaking up over the horizon and was a welcome sight to the group, as they marvelled in the sheer majesty of the early dawn.

The return down the mountain was uneventful and peaceful, just as it had been before. The wind was much less antagonistic compared to the day before, as the group high-stepped over the terrain in some spots, and used their hiking poles to help lessen the strain of movement at the higher elevation. Fred would occasionally take breaks with the others, but Sam had to make himself stop, not feeling anywhere as winded as he was yesterday at the high elevation.

"Sam, what the hell?" Fred jested in between breaths. You get into one fight, and now you're moving like Superman. Are you sure you're okay?" Sam hadn't noticed until Fred said something, but he was right. Turning to Fred, he replied, "This is going to sound weird, but I feel incredible. I don't feel too tired. Maybe the hike up is worse than down?"

"Acclimation, maybe? But that's fast for acclimation," Donte added. Sam shrugged his shoulders and took a few minutes with the others, before they resumed the descent. Sam was brimming with energy the whole day. He had experience in running track, but that was high school, three years back. Now, why so much vitality? He hadn't worked out since he graduated high school and took the summer off to relax. His awareness felt as on point as it

had ever been, as well. The trek was little more than an
inconvenience, while the others showed signs of struggle against it.
Within the next handful of hours, they made it back down to where
they came the day prior, and all stretched. Donte looked around
and saw that Bradley's car was gone.
"Hey fellas, Bradley's car isn't here. I think he somehow made it
down the mountain last night and split," he informed the others.
The rest of the group glanced at where his car had been, and
inquisitive looks took hold of their faces, wondering just exactly
where and why Bradley left. Sam said to Donte, "Maybe he headed
back to campus?" Donte replied, "I don't care what he did, that
was jacked up what he pulled last night."

"What a guy," Fred remarked, his tone and facial expression showing one of disdain. "Hazes new initiates, gets his ass kicked, runs off." Sam broke up the tension and said, "Why don't we head back to campus and grab dinner? He'll surely show up or be back there when we return." The others had no quarrel with the plan proposed and got in their vehicles to head back.

Over the span of the next couple of hours, Fred and Sam were discussing the events of the night before, still trying to grasp all that transpired.

"Dude, I don't get it," Fred said, eyes ahead on the road. "That weird flash of light, the giant bone, Bradley taking off: it's all so confusing. I don't know what we happened across, but I'd rather not think about it too much." Sam nodded, taking a swig of water, gazing upon the evening sky. The sun was once again setting into the horizon, which was a soothing, welcome sight compared to the events that transpired the night before on Mount Elbert. Swallowing the gulp, Sam replied, "Some initiation, huh? Hey, we're Sigma Pi now, at least!"

Fred shook his head with a smile, saying, "You've always been a guy of silver linings." Sam cracked the window a bit to let the cold Colorado air in and refresh his senses. The crisp, mountainous air was even more intoxicating than before, as Sam breathed deeply of the lovely air. He thought that he could smell trace scents in the wind: grill smoke, lake waters, even the faint scent of laundered clothes hanging to dry outside in the passing towns. He continued taking it all in, feeling full of life.

"Hey Sam," Fred said, glancing to his side. "What are you doing?" Sam came out of his reverie of analysing all the scents, realizing he must have looked a bit silly to Fred. Rubbing the back of his head and with a sheepish grin on his face, he replied, "I was...smelling the air. I smelled so many scents. The nice dry smoke off a grill, the lakes, even clean clothes!" Fred paused for a moment, then replied, "Uh...are you *sure* you're okay? What are you? Superhuman now?" Sam shrugged his shoulders, then replied, "I don't know, man." Letting the sentiment hang in the air for a moment, he then said, "You don't think last night...that something happened to me, do you?"

Fred replied, "I'm not sure. That light was weird as hell, but I don't take stock in the supernatural, or anything like that. Maybe you should get checked." Sam looked at his hands, inspecting them. The bruising and abrasions from the fighting last night seemed to have faded and healed greatly, with only minor marks left on them.

"Yeah. Maybe I'm just being crazy. I don't ever want to do another séance in my life again though. Especially atop a mountain in the middle of nowhere." Fred pursed his lips for a moment and added, "Agreed. That was something else. But it's behind us now. If we see Bradley again, I'm sure Donte will have words with him. The guys weren't cool with seeing how panicked you were, and me stopping Bradley going after you."

"He went after me?!" Sam asked, bewildered. Fred shot back, "Yeah! Did you not see him heading to you, with that creepy ass look on his face?" Sam shook his head and muttered back, "No...I was in some sort of trance at that point. It's like the air got heavy, and my head was foggy and swimming with whispers that became voices. I can't explain it exactly, but it was as though the world was getting tuned out and a darkness was pulling me in. Like the night just suddenly crashed upon us." Fred briefly glanced to Sam, a concerned look on his face and replied, "Sam, maybe you should get checked out. That's just weird. I can say I'm genuinely worried about you now." Sam looked out his window and replied, "I'm sorry for scaring you. You're right, maybe I'm just being weird. Either way, Bradley will answer for what he did. Donte and the others aren't happy about it." Fred said, "Yeah, they're not. Let's focus on getting to SRV Steakhouse and getting some dinner with them first. I'm sure we can talk there more, as well as tear into some real food."

By dusk, the stars were coming out against the darkening sky as Fred parked the jeep. Getting out, the two young men made their way inside and were greeted by the faces of their fellow Sigma Pi members.

Making their way to the table where their fellow fraternity brothers were, Fred and Sam sat down and saw a beer awaiting each one as they did. Sara was working again that night, and was delighted at seeing not only the Sigma Pi group, but Sam as well. Fred would tell the others about how shy he was, and jested of Sam's first encounter with her, prompting laughter from the group. Stories were told amongst all the members to better get to know one another, and toasts to Sam and Fred joining the fraternity were given all around.

"Sam over here has been on some weird stuff since we've returned from the mountain," Fred jested, taking a swig of his beer. "I never in my life have seen him move like he did on the mountain when he took on Bradley. I mean, he's done soccer before, but that's about it."

"Quick feet bro, that's how he got the fists in so quick," Donte added as the table erupted into laughter. Sam felt his ears burning red as Fred continued, "I'm honestly stoked, though. Bradley's a dick, I was happy to watch that. He had been doing sketchy stuff since being president, like using fundraiser support to buy a new car, or hazing the freshman girls that come. Yet, here comes Sam, all quiet and whatnot, until they scuffle. Instant beast! Then, today, Sam makes his way down the mountain like a pro hiker, barely breaking a sweat and even smelling the air like a wolf, saying he's smelling all these scents in the wind. That light at the mountain must've been something."

The group thought on it in silence for a moment as Sara approached the table and asked, "Sounds like you fellas had a fantastic time on Mount Elbert. Congrats to you both by the way,

Fred and Sam!" Donte put his burger down, looked to Sara and replied, "Some weird stuff happened. Bradley tried sticking Fred, Sam got mad, beat his ass, a giant light flashed, and we all blacked out. I know it sounds like we were drunk, but we weren't."
Sara's face twisted with surprise, as she ruminated on what Donte had said. Turning to Sam, he added, "It's true. He hit Fred, I hit him back. Then there was some flash of light and the next thing we know, we're on the ground." Sara looked at all the guys, and each one had a serious expression on their faces.
"Well...that sounds like it was scary. You boys probably shouldn't be going out to places like that and trying to chant on things you don't know about." Donte shot back, "Sara, what the hell do you know about spooky stuff?" Sara put a hand on her hip, and with a smirk,

replied, "Surprisingly, a decent amount. I know to not go on mountain tops and perform seances, or to use Ouija boards. Oh, I also know to respect burial grounds." The table got quiet and Donte's face went still with horror, the veiled remark not lost on him.

"That's...a burial ground?!" he asked, a shiver taking him over. Sara grinned and said back, "So legends go. My grandfather told me things about that mountain. I wouldn't go messing with it." With that, she returned to making her rounds around the restaurant. The rest of the fraternity sat in silence for a moment until another spoke up and said, "Donte, you looked pretty scared there. You okay?" The table burst into laughter as Donte shook his head and went back to eating his burger.

Chapter 6: Adjustment

A week had passed since the night of the induction, and the Sigma Pi members were at ease again, going about their classes and preparing for the upcoming Halloween party they planned to throw. Donte went to the school administration and inquired where Bradley had been. No one had seen him since, professor, dean or student. It wasn't until the end of that very week that one of the administrative staff members informed Sigma Pi that Bradley had written a letter to the school, stating that he had transferred and taken leave. Donte later passed the news to the rest of the Sigma Pi house, which was mostly met with warm reception. One of the members, a computer science student named Ben Longhaus said, "Well, that means you're now president of the fraternity now, Donte!"

The house went up in loud cheers and cries, celebrating the appointment of their new fraternity president, which was followed by celebratory beers. The Sigma Pi house itself had two floors, with stone rocks making up the wall, and wooden beams lining up on the ceiling to give the interior a rustic look, as though it were a hunting lodge. Couches were neatly arranged around a coffee table in the living room, where a brick fireplace had a cosy fire crackling at the centre. Across the room, there was a kitchen that was surprisingly well stocked with food to cook. Donte handled food and electricity during his tenure as vice president, and believed the guys should all know how to cook their own meals to help save on the budget.

Though initially not fond of cooking, the Sigma Pi members came to like it, even going the extra step to hunt game and fish for food, thus getting a reputation as one of the most outdoorsy houses in Keystone Hall University. The school itself was a relatively small place, compared to bigger institutions and in turn, the houses were built smaller to accommodate the fewer number of students in kind.

Sam and Fred preferred keeping their normal dorm, the cabin-esque quarters, a little further from campus, but spent more time around the Sigma Pi house since getting inducted. The days passed until Halloween came, which meant Sigma Pi throwing an extravagant party. The usual fare of various costumes, liquor bottles, beer cases, kegs, and other substances made their way around the party.

Sam didn't dress in costume on that night, instead wearing a pair of grey jeans and a blue shirt. He played rounds of chess against various people at one of the smaller tables in the commons area. What Sam's opponents didn't know was that he was an avid chess player, and he effortlessly swept five opponents in a row. Fred had always known but preferred to let others find out first-hand, much to his amusement.

The day after, most of the Sigma Pi house shook off their lingering hangovers from the night before, and geared up to go hunting; something that Sam had never done before. Fred had a date with one of the campus girls and opted out of the day trip, as Sam loaded up with one of the members named Steve McOrwell, a short blond-haired guy with a stocky build, green eyes and rugged features that often drew the attention of the women on campus. The two followed a few of the others with their gear, as they made their way to an open stretch of land where elk were often seen.

Two hours later, Steve and Sam were sitting against a rock, amidst a plain of shin-high grass. Looking through the metal ring of his crossbow scope, Sam said, "Wow. I've never shot one of these before. It's as simple as aiming and firing?"

"It's that simple, bub," Steve replied, his Midwest accent on display. "Back home in Minnesota, my pops taught me on crossbow as a kid before he moved me to guns." Sam took a moment to admire the craftsmanship of the weapon, with its camouflage paint scheme across a sturdy metal body. The grip was tailored to comfortably dig into the hand, helping to keep a hold of the crossbow. The scope had a row of notches on the right side, to gauge elevation and distance needed to better hit the target. As Sam was taking note of every detail, Steve tapped his shoulder and pointed ahead.

Peering over the rock, a large deer with a grey and brown coat was grazing on the grass across the field. Its rack was impressive, antlers jutting out from both sides. Its jaw was coated white and easily stood double the height of a human. Sam felt a rush of blood just looking at the deer, as his mouth began to salivate. His attention to detail became more acute, noticing the mild wind direction from behind the two, and the deer's movements. The buck was an impressive size, its neck and legs thick with bulky muscles built over the course of traversing vast terrain, and proportionately huge amounts of food.

Steve went into a prone position with his loaded crossbow and belly crawled up a couple feet. Sam loaded a bolt up before joining Steve. Taking out a pair of binoculars, Steve peered into them, his focus on the game ahead. Whispering to Sam, he said, "Okay bud, by my guess, he's fifty yards out. We've got to move slowly with making as little racquet as possible. Ready?" Sam nodded and got to his feet with Steve, beginning to close the distance with painstakingly slow movement and extra caution to footsteps. Minutes felt like hours as the two gradually closed the gap on the prize they sought. Steve pressed down into the dirt as Sam judged how much closer the massive buck was. Steve began to line up a shot and took position to fire. His bolt was let loose and caught the deer in its flank. Immediately snorting and turning around, it began to make a dash as Sam witnessed the whole event in what he perceived as slow motion. Springing to his feet, Sam dashed

forward to get an ideal shot lined up, and took off for the large
target.
The buck reared up on its hind legs and tried to pivot and turn,
showing the side of its impressive chest: Sam saw his opportunity.
He immediately knelt, brought the crossbow up and squeezed the
trigger. A click was heard as the bolt left the weapon and sailed
true to the deer, piercing it in the chest. Blood immediately gushed
from the wound and came in pulses: Steve saw that Sam had hit
the mark right in the deer's vitals. The deer staggered in confusion,
curious as to what just hit it. Blood was splattering to the ground
as it made a dash to escape. The massive quarry ran a good
distance before finally giving way to the shot and dropping.

Sam and Steve made their way to the fallen buck, which Steve calculated to be a good one hundred and twenty-two yards from their original position. Coming up to their kill, the buck was even more impressive up close. With its rugged fur coat, the large animal's head was easily near double the size of each of theirs. The antlers were jagged and formed upward, as if reaching to the sky by the grace of nature's majesty. Blood matted the fur in the haunch where Steve hit it, and in the chest where Sam made his shot. Looking at both shots, Steve whistled and exclaimed, "Sam, that was a shot right through the heart! Textbook aim right behind the front leg upper joint! You sure you never used these before?" Sam looked dumbfounded at the deer, astonished at what Steve just told him. He shrugged and replied, "I don't know...it's like I just had the instinct to shoot him there, like I could almost feel his heartbeat in the moment." Steve looked to Sam and remarked, "Whenever I go hunting, I'm bringing you. You're a natural. Now, let's go get the sled and bring this big guy back, so we can eat some venison tonight." Steve took another look at Sam's mark, still amazed at how well his aim was.

Sam left the area to head back and retrieve the sled. Upon grabbing it from their vehicle, he took it back and helped Steve load the deer on to it. It was quite heavy, an easy ten-point buck from what Steve discerned. The two worked arduously for a few minutes to lift the deer on, then after doing so, headed back to Steve's pickup. The two then began working to load the deer onto the dropped tailgate, and with some coordination and effort, both Sam and Steve got the buck on, as Steve lifted and secured the tailgate. As the two got in, Sam's ear caught the distinct sound of a large cat's growl across the field. His eyes darted around as he felt his senses go into hyperawareness, trying to pinpoint the location. "Steve, did you hear that?" Sam asked, his nerves on edge. Starting the truck, Steve replied, "No, what did you hear?" Sam, staring around the field, replied, "A cat. A big one. I feel like it knows we're here and is trying to hunt us." Steve started backing out and then putting the vehicle into drive, replied, "Probably a mountain lion. We've got those out here. Good hearing, because I sure as heck heard nothing." Sam made a note to himself of mountain lions and took a breath, feeling somewhat relieved, but strangely on edge as if it were calling out to them. To him." The two made their way back to campus and would spend the rest of the day skinning, cleaning and getting the meat off their magnificent prize.

Chapter 7: Spots of a Different Breed

In the hollow space of a stone room, the cool chill of the air seeped in, as torches sat snugly on iron sconces of the walls. Orange light glowed and flickered tempestuously, as a slender, tall, young man walked beside another, one with bronze skin, shoulder-length black hair, and dark brown eyes that seemed to pierce through the spirit of anyone who looked his way. He sported the heavy pelt of an elk, with a garb of vibrantly coloured robes, golden bracers on his wrists, and a blood-red sash tied firmly around his waist. Corded muscles enveloped his form and only further enhanced his powerful frame, despite the younger man next to him standing taller.

The younger man, visibly unsettled by the man next to him, meekly said, "W-who...are you?" The man in colorful regalia smirked, and replied with a deep, silky voice, "Why, I am the forerunner of the long-forgotten order of our kind."

"Our kind?" the young man asked.

"Yes," the man replied with a small nod of his head. "You and I, we're of the same kind now. How do you think you made it here?"

"I don't know." The young man held a curious palm facing upwards and continued, "All I recall was a great light, then nothing." The garbed man laughed a bit, then said, "You set me free, along with the spirits of the others. What I'm about to tell you will surpass your immediate understanding, so try not to hold too much doubt when I tell you."

The two reached the opening of a room that had a round table, with empty chairs surrounding it. The room had the scent of burning incense wafting in the air from the burner, with lit braziers of hot coals. The man waved his hand to the table, inviting the young man to sit. He did as such, as the two pulled chairs out and sat down at the table. Looking around the room, the taller of the two asked, "Wh-where is this? What is this?"

The garbed man cleared his throat and began to speak. Looking to the younger man, he said, "This is an abandoned hideout of an old order, one of humans and wyverns." The young man tilted his head, puzzlement taking his face over. Bewildered, he asked, "Wyverns? Like dragons?" The man nodded and replied, "The very same."

The young man took a double take from sheer confusion, astounded at the older man's mention of dragons. As farfetched as his tale started, he somehow felt like the man was telling the truth. The man continued, "I told you this would not be an easy tale to swallow. The order of the two came together some time ago, when the Jan Damis roamed the lands. The Jan Damis were a group of people that bore the ability to shapeshift into leopards, as well as gain some of their senses and latent abilities.

"In the times of old, the Jan Damis formed a secret society to make the world a better place. They worked behind the scenes with governments, various nations and people to shape reality to their will. The Jan Damis also hunted their mortal enemy, the wyverns, with ruthless efficiency. However, one day that changed with the alliance that came to be.

"A group of humans led by a famous soldier and explorer found the means to seal their powers away. Teaming up with the last of the wyverns, the two races made an alliance to stop the Jan Damis from achieving their destiny. At first, a few were found and hunted down. However, interrogations on some of their captives led to giving away more and more of the positions in which the Jan Damis laid in hiding." The young man, jaw hanging open, stared for a moment before replying, "That's horrible! The Jan Damis wanted to make the world better! And what did they get for their efforts? Being hunted down?"

"Yes, I understand how you feel, young one," the man replied, a knowing smile taking form. "They were captured and even slaughtered to the man when the campaign was led against them. One by one, they fell to death or had their abilities sealed away. Eventually, they found the hideout of the Jan Damis and waged one last battle against them. The Jan Damis fell and had their powers sealed for many years. However, I strongly believe they've awakened again."

The young man leaned in and asked, "How do you know?" The man leaned in as well and purred, "Why, because I was there, *mijo.*" The young man looked absolutely flabbergasted as he shot back in disbelief, "No way. I think the story has gone too far now." The man smiled and said, "Maybe this will change your mind." Standing up out of his seat, the garbed man stared at the young man and watched his surprised reaction, his dark eyes beginning to glow yellow, with the pupils becoming a slit. An undercurrent of lethality rumbled in his deep voice, "Do you believe me now?"

The young man then watched the man shift into a large leopard before him, with a dark sheen of fur and spots all around. Muscles rippled underneath the fur and wrapped around the body of the large cat, as sharp teeth glistened from a maw of power. The tail flickered fickly, curling and unfurling in a series of unpredictable flicks. Large claws scratched the stone floor, making uncomfortable noises on the surface. His voice became a rumbling, a purr of the cat of the hunt. The leopard walked to the young man and let out a low growl, setting the young man on edge. Suddenly, the leopard reverted to a human figure: it was the same man as before. Smiling, he asked, "Do you believe me now?"

"I...yes! Yes, I do!" the young man blurted, clearly afraid for his life." The man sat back down and explained, "Please, have no worry. I have use for you. I'd like you to become my first apprentice. The first I've had in many years." The young man relaxed a bit, his fear now transmuting into growing curiosity."

"Apprentice?"
"Yes, an apprentice."
"What does it entail?"
"You learn to harness your ability and we'll begin to find others to join our cause."
"My ability?! I have it?!" the young man asked, shifting back into confusion. The man laughed and replied, "Yes. When you unsealed me that night on the mountain, you absorbed one of the essences that granted the power." The young man nearly fell out of his chair, beyond

all belief by then. He gathered himself, then asked, "How did I gain this? Do you mean when that flash of light happened?"

"Yes. That was the night you freed me, as well as let loose the seal. It seems that I was most fortunate in you finding me." The man pulled out a talisman of interlocking squares in the design, which glowed upon being held up. "By the way, what's your name, *amigo?*"

"Bradley, sir. I was on a camping trip with some friends and there was a fight. Next thing I know, I'm waking up in here." The man nodded, his silence an indication of his digestion of the information. He then said, "I see, Bradley. My name is Rodrigo de la Muerte, former king of a civilization blessed with the power of the leopard. You now have the gift as well, according to this seal, the Oro Luna." Holding the talisman up, a crimson glow began to emanate from it, before turning orange and pulsing. Nodding, Rodrigo said, "I see. You have the essence of a former war chief. You've got great potential for your ability."

"You can tell just from that thing what...essence I have?"

"I can indeed. You have the essence of an old war chief of mine. Essences that stand a cut above the normal ones will show accordingly. My, Bradley, you're quite lucky." Bradley began to ponder Rodrigo's words as the king continued, "You may not know everything yet, but I will teach you all you need to know. How to hunt, how to shift, how to be everything you could be and more." Bradley was liking everything he heard and had cast out any doubts in his mind by now, convinced with all he saw.

"I want to learn, leopard king," Bradley said with a tone of respect. The garbed man shook his head and replied, "I appreciate the respect, but please, call me Rodrigo. It was you who had set me free, after all. My civilization is probably long gone, by now. I'm nothing more than king of this simple talisman." Getting up, he beckoned for Bradley to follow him. He did so, leaving his chair and following Rodrigo. Passing through the halls, the two eventually came upon a large entrance to an empty cavern, one which was man-made from the look of it. The cavern was well-cut and worn, formed in a circle, with inscriptions on the wall. Bradley asked Rodrigo, "What is this?"

"My friend," Rodrigo began, "This is the cavern of awakening. Here, we will begin to train you up in your ability and skills, to make you a truly fearsome adversary to any who would stand in your way. Bradley thought for a moment, recalling the night he and Sam fought atop Mount Elbert. Sam easily overpowered him and embarrassed him in front of his fraternity. The Fraternity!

They were probably wondering where he was. Bradley shook the
thought from his mind, his focus now completely on the cavern.
He had powers. The ability to shapeshift into a leopard!
Rodrigo could see the glint of excitement in his eyes and began to
explain more. Clearing his throat, he said, "Look around here,
Bradley. This was once a hideout for the alliance that stopped the
Jan Damis. Now, we will repurpose it for our own needs. In the
week you've been unconscious, I've looked after you and made the
place our own. How fitting an irony, that we should use the place
of our once adversaries to our liking!" Bradley, despite barely
having any light in the cavern, could see better than normal.

"Rodrigo...I can almost see in this low light!" he exclaimed. "You're right! I must have the power to transform into a leopard!" Rodrigo smiled and said, "Why yes, that's your basic senses being heightened by the leopard essence within you! You will grow used to it, as well as having quicker reflexes, a heightened sense of smell, endurance, and increased want for the hunt." Bradley felt his stomach rumble as hunger began to wash over him. Rodrigo laughed and said, "You must be starving after your slumber. Come, let us go outside and hunt our food."

Bradley and Rodrigo walked outside to the sun setting in the mountains. Rodrigo shifted into his leopard and watched, indicating he wanted Bradley to do the same. Bradley felt a tug inside him, as if another being was within his body. Feeling his senses greatly heighten, his mouth began to water for food, for a kill. His perspective grew closer to the ground as he felt his body go on all fours. As if it were second nature to him, Bradley looked at his hands, only to find paws.

"Oh man! I'm a leopard! This is actually real!" Bradley thought, scanning the outside. He felt a preternatural awareness of his surroundings, as well as a connection to Rodrigo as the larger, dark leopard led the smaller one. The two ran off into the night as the wind hit Bradley's face. He was amazed at how quickly he moved, how agile he was, how *alive* he was. The air carried new scents as he ran at breakneck speed with Rodrigo, making his way down the mountains with unparalleled swiftness.

The two made it to the bottom and began seeking prey to hunt. Rodrigo crouched low behind a boulder as Bradley followed suit. The scent of wild game immediately caught their attention as a deer was grazing in the fields ahead. The two crept across the soft grass with painstaking care to not alert their quarry. Time seemed to slow down as Bradley felt his body instinctively grow tense with coiled tension and bloodlust. The two lowered their frames again, and Bradley waited on Rodrigo to give the signal. Rodrigo got up into a prance, then sprung into a sprint that caught the deer off guard. Trying to run, Rodrigo managed to claw a hind leg and hold on. Bradley soon came in with a lethal strike at its neck. Blood splashed from the wound and Bradley gave in to the hunt as he tore into the neck of the large game. It didn't take long for the deer to drop dead.

Rodrigo shifted back into human form as Bradley did the same. In the trance-like state of the hunt, Bradley cried, "Why did we stop?! Let's eat!!!" Rodrigo laughed, bringing Bradley back to his senses as he replied, "We can eat it raw, or cook it and prepare it to be even more delicious. I know this is new to you, but I promise its better cooked. We're still human, after all." Bradley felt a warm fluid around his mouth, wiped it away and saw it was fresh blood. The sight startled him, as well as what he just said to Rodrigo. The leopard king looked to Bradley and said, "Don't be ashamed. It's part of the process. Come, let's haul this back to the mountain and enjoy a fine dinner."

Chapter 8: Malicious Mentorship

The two managed to bring their game back to the mountain hideout they had found, and began to clean and skin the large deer, before placing it on a spit and roasting it. The scent of grilled meat hung in the air with a potent scent of roasted meat, the kind to make any human or beast salivate upon smelling. Bradley waited for a few minutes before taking a generous slice of meat off the leg and tearing into it. The first bite tasted like the most delicious thing he had ever had in his life. The flavor of the deer seemed raw, yet abnormally natural to consume. The warm meat had a slight smoked taste to it, only further driving Bradley's taste buds wild. Was it supposed to taste this good? Had it always been this natural to crave meat this badly? Bradley waved the questions aside, hungrily tearing into the kill that the two got. As Rodrigo cut him a slice off the flank, he said to Bradley, "Fine work for your first shift. It's as though it were natural."

Swallowing a sizable piece, Bradley replied, "It felt like I had done it all my life. As though my body knew what to do when we went after that deer. It's like...I had been a jaguar all my life...and yet, I'm still human." Rodrigo nodded, taking a small bite before he replied, "It will feel like that. Having the essence of the leopard in you, means you gain the abilities and use them as though you were born as the cat. Each essence is different, mind you. Some essences you gain grant the leopard abilities to a base extent. Some carry memories of those who wielded the essence, of which you may end up experiencing. Some even provide a normal skill a human normally wouldn't have, just to suddenly be able to do so."

"How do you mean?" Bradley asked.

"Say you have never swam before or lacked the ability to do. That essence may have come from someone who swam with no problem. By taking on the essence, you may then have access to that person's former skill," Rodrigo replied, taking another small bite of deer meat.

Bradley slowly nodded his head, the concept starting to make sense to him. He said to Rodrigo, "That's incredible. Just incredible." The two continued to eat their dinner in silence for a few minutes, until Bradley asked another question.

"With reawakening, what do you plan to do?"

"What do I plan to do, you ask," Rodrigo replied. Looking Bradley in the eyes with a stare that could unnerve the mightiest of men, he spoke, "I plan to form another order. Much like the Jan Damis once existed, except maybe on a smaller scale. I still need to acclimate to the times, in which it seems lots of it has passed. Around the time you helped release me with some of the other essences, I carried you back to this hideout to let you recover. I felt nearly a dozen presences on that mountaintop that night. You ended up reciting the chant of awakening, and with a bit of blood over the talisman, released the seal on me, as well as other essences."

Bradley thought for a moment, then asked, "Does this mean other people have essences too? I was up there with my fraternity that night and got into a scuffle with one of the new guys. Do the others have it too?" Rodrigo immediately replied to him, "There's one. That night, I detected

no other essences except one. I wasn't sure, and having just
reawakened, I was still vulnerable enough. I took you here in the
hopes we would both recover, which we did. I've still yet to fully
recover my full powers, due to the sheer amount of time being
locked away in the Oro Luna."
"Who was the one that you detected?"
"It was a young man, with a timid soul that found ferocity in the
heat of the moment. I felt his anger and need to protect, draw one
of the essences into him."
"Sam," Bradley muttered, his suspicions being raised. Rodrigo
continued, "If you mean the dark haired one, then yes. He was one
of two that didn't wear the same outfit as you all, right?" Bradley
nodded, as a knot formed in his stomach and his ears began to
grow hot. Looking to Rodrigo with a serious glance, he asked, "Are
you sure?"
"I am. He revisited the lands earlier with a friend to hunt their own
food. I came down the mountain to see where the essence was.
Indeed, the boy has the power as well." Bradley clenched a fist, and
snarled, "That damn newbie. He came to town and wanted to be a
Sigma Pi member so badly. We make this grand hike, and then he
wants to fight me for simply getting his friend to calm down. Not
only that but embarrassing me in front of my fraternity!"
"Oh ho!" Rodrigo said with a grin and less-than-kind look in his
eyes. "It seems this Sam fellow has your ire! Tell me more about
him!"
Bradley tore off another bite of deer meat from the bone and said,
"He came from Florida to attend college here. The fraternity
members kept hyping him and his friend up as they settled in here.
At first, I was happy to bring them on. But over time, they started
to see them as a welcome addition and replacement to my
headship of the fraternity. They would speak about how those two
was going to change things, how Sam would be a great president of
the house, how we need to stop the mountain ritual that we'd
perform. And look! It brought us these wonderful powers, as well
as brought you back to life! Sam himself even started moving in on
the girl I've been talking to for the last few years I've been here!
She doesn't give me the time of day, and yet he hits things off with
her no problem!"
Rodrigo observed with great perceptive intensity as Bradley went
on about his vendetta with Sam, culminating in the fight on top of
Mount Elbert. When Bradley finished, Rodrigo stared for a
moment in silence before he responded, "I see. You have come to
detest this competition with the new blood in your ranks, yes?"

Bradley nodded. Rodrigo continued, "Then, if he's such a threat, perhaps you need to seek battle with him again, let him know you're no longer to be trifled with." Bradley smiled at the thought, and replied, "Yeah, I could use a rematch against him! As far as I'm concerned, we're far from done."
Rodrigo said to Bradley, his voice flipping from playful to commanding, "Then finish your dinner. Once you do, we're going to begin your training." Bradley jumped, startled from the sudden switch as he fumbled in his reply, "Um...uh, okay! But what are we going to do?" Rodrigo replied with stone cold tonality, "You're going to grow your skills as a leopard shifter. I need a strong second to help me gather up a new order of shifters. Starting with us two, we will continue what the Jan Damis had long left behind."

"I will do anything you ask, Rodrigo. My main concern is getting even with Sam."

"That's good, *mijo*. I wish to establish a much smaller order, one that can move with far less interference, with less risk for captivity. I don't wish to repeat what led to the initial fall of the Jan Damis. Together, we will indeed bring it back, however."

"How do you plan to do that?"

"With this." Rodrigo held up the Oro Luna, as it glowed crimson. "This seal will help detect others like ourselves."

"How many are there?"

"The original essences were a total of five. Each essence was split to give to others, effectively increasing their numbers, but diminishing their strength. You and Sam have two of them already. That means excluding myself, there's three more out there. Where? I'm not sure, but the Oro Luna here will help us locate them all. I plan to leave this hideout after your...initiation and training, to seek the others out."

"What do you need me to do?"

"Bide your time. Prepare. When it is time to reclaim the essence your old rival has, I will say so." Bradley jumped up and blustered, "I can take him now! Let me go find him and take the essence." Rodrigo held a hand up, calmly replying, "Patience. As of currently, you'd stand little chance against him, let alone take his essence. You don't even know how to do that."

"I feel like I can beat him!" Rodrigo glared at him with glowing yellow eyes, prompting Bradley to check his enthusiasm. He then said, "You don't even know how to take essence. As it stands, Sam has the edge on you in terms of skill. While he hasn't shown his shift familiarity, he soundly beat you with the senses on the mountain top alone. His essence seems to react to the stress he's in, which no doubt is likely the essence of the iron shaman."

"The what?" Bradley asked, confused. Rodrigo took a breath then replied, "Each essence originates from a user of my old tribe. You bear the essence that my war chief once did. The fire scout, spirit shaman and tribe hunter are currently out there. Sam bears the essence of the iron shaman, a person who has walked a line between serenity and stoic battle prowess. The war chief and he were the two strongest of the tribe."

Bradley sat on the piece of information given for a time, before he finally asked, "I see. And Sam and I now possess the essences of both of those two, right? Well...then I guess you're right. We'll gather the others first. I'll train. My question now is...how does one take an essence?"

Rodrigo held up two fingers, and replied, "The two ways most accessible to us are as follows: one, by using the Oro Luna to seal it. This was how the Jan Damis met their end." Bradley asked, "What's the other?" Rodrigo put his hand down, building the suspense for Bradley. With a casual reply, Rodrigo answered, "Death."

Bradley's face went a bit pale at the sound of that. Sure, he hated
Sam somewhat fiercely. But killing him? Bradley wasn't sure about
that part." Rodrigo caught on to his blanching at the word and
laughed an unsettling laugh, and said, "Now, death obviously is an
extreme. BUT," catching Bradley's attention even more with the
inflection change, "But if we must do so, so be it." Turning to face
one of the stone corridors, Rodrigo said, "Now, they can also go
through the sacred incantation to draw it out. Come with me.
Down this way, I want to show you the remains of some history
you need to know about."
The two began down the stone passageway with Bradley's nerves
on edge. Everything he just learned: it was so intoxicating, but also
terrifying at the same time. He wanted to fight Sam again, but kill
him? Wasn't that a bit inhumane? Then again, didn't he just get
done savouring the hunt of the deer they found? The thoughts
swirled in his head and only went away when they arrived at an
open area. What Bradley saw made his jaw drop yet again: there
was the massive skeleton of something that looked like a winged
dinosaur. Rodrigo looked to him and said, "Behold! The remains of
one of the wyverns of yore!"

Chapter 9: A Cold Winter

A couple of months had passed, and many of the students had gone home to spend time with loved ones for the Christmas break. Since Halloween, Sam and Sara had been talking more, as well as hanging out in between classes. He found out that Sara was going to be an environmental engineer, which only furthered his interest in her. Sam learned over the months that she was born in Iceland, and had moved to Colorado when she was young. Her family helped run the SRV Steakhouse that apparently belonged to a family friend, which had been open for quite some time.

Upon returning from his visit to Florida, Fred opted to stay behind another week to catch up with his father. Many of the Sigma Pi members were also on vacation, which left Sam more time to spend with Sara. The two would go hiking through many of the trails she knew of, as well as snowboarding at the local resort. The Keystone resort was filled with white, snowy slopes and the lifts carried skiers and snowboarders across the ways. Sam and Sara strapped in their own boards and hit the slopes upon arrival. Sam had never snowboarded in his life, but displayed a natural prowess, having little trouble standing up and riding the slopes. Sara was impressed that he took to it so quickly, and the two spent the day kicking up the snowy powder, taking in the sights and riding until they were too sore to continue. By evening, the two turned in their rentals and switched back to their normal outfits, before deciding to go to a dinner at one of the resort restaurants there.

As Sara and Sam sat down, the waiter came to take their orders and left, leaving the two be. It was a quiet, moderately upscale place, with crisp tablecloths neatly ironed and pressed, with candles at the centre of the table, giving the white cloth a glow of warmth. The lights were dim and were complimented by the icicle lights hung around for the holidays, as customers of various ages all enjoyed some sort of meal or fancy cocktails, with gentle piano music playing in the background.

Sara looked to Sam and said with a mirthful smile, "Sam, I didn't know you knew how to snowboard like that."

"Honestly, neither did I," he sheepishly replied. "It came naturally once I got the standing up part down." Sara giggled before replying, "Ever so humble." Sam returned her glance with more focus as he said to her, "It's weird. I can't quite explain it, but since the initiation up on the mountain, I feel more...alive."

"Maybe it's the accomplishment of having made that hike?"

"Maybe so. But my body just seems more focused, like I gained superpowers." Sara looked at him quizzically, before asking with a hint of hesitation, "Sam, what exactly happened up there that night?"

Sam looked up in thought, then replied, "Well, it happened like this. And please don't think of me as a weirdo for this, since I've got several witnesses that saw the same thing. But we climbed

the mountain, right? We made it to the top, which is when Bradley
wanted to start doing a séance. Everyone starts chanting and…I
feel this wave of approaching darkness come over me. Everything
got heavy." Sam held his hands up to his head, fingers outstretched
as he continued, "As if the air grew solid and began to push on me.
During the chanting, Fred got up to stop Bradley, and the two
started fighting. Seeing it happen, I went to stop Bradley,
especially after he hit Fred. He then hits me, and it's like I woke up
from the haze. Everything happened in lucid, slow motion, as I saw
myself naturally avoiding every punch that he could throw at me"
Sam held his hands up, curled them into fists and recreated the
slow movements he saw to Sara, as he explained, "I never had been
in a fight in my life but at that moment, it's like I just knew what to
do. Well, I ended up knocking him down as a bright yellow light
shone hard enough to knock us all out. After that, nothing. At
least, until we woke up and Bradley was gone. Apparently, he
transferred shortly after that."
Sara was staring intently, with undivided attention as Sam
nervously said, "Uh, did I say something wrong?" Sara held her
gaze for a moment before replying, "Sam, there's a local legend
around here that Mount Elbert held something powerful. I don't
know how much you buy into stories like that, but that sounds very
much like the legend of something buried away there."
"How do you know?"
Sara took a breath, then spoke, "When I was young, my dad told
me our family line has lived in Colorado for generations. We have
pictures of my great-great grandfather at some sort of weird
temple in a jungle somewhere. He apparently moved to Colorado,
which is where my family line on my dad's side comes from. My
great-great grandfather was a researcher of some sort, but never
fully explained to me by my dad. He'd always avoid the questions.
My grandfather however, used to tell me tales that apparently in
the world, there were people who could change into animals."
Sam looked wildly at her as she said, "I know it sounds dumb, but I
liked the stories as a kid!" Sam shook his head and said, "No, it's
not that. I feel like your grandfather was maybe right on
something." Stopping to pause for a moment, he looked down at
the table in thought, then back to her and asked, "Sara, do you
think what he told you may be true?" Sara shook her head and
abruptly changed the topic as she said, "Why don't we talk about
something else?" Sam immediately replied, "Sure! I didn't mean to
make you uncomfortable. Hey, you look really nice for having

spent a day on the slopes!" Sara laughed and replied, "That's
better."

The two enjoyed a nice, cosy dinner at the restaurant, and when
the time came to leave, Sam paid the bill as the two left.

Walking out to Sara's car, the two got in and drove off down the
road. They started making their way for a spot that had a flat rock,
where they could be alone and look up at the clear winter sky. The
headlights eventually lit up a boulder with a portion of the top
missing, as the car made a turn for it and drove up to it. Parking
and shutting it off, the two got out and stood before the large
boulder. It was a few inches up over their heads to get to, and Sam
pulled out a lantern from his backpack, set it down, then clasped
his fingers together to give Sara a boost onto the rock. Once up
there, Sam followed suit by finding a few footholds and pulling
himself up.

Setting the lantern down, he turned the knob off and the light went out. Once both of their eyes adjusted, a majestic spread of starlit sky and a full moon hung above them, shining a gentle glow back down on them. Laying on his back, Sam took a deep breath and said, "Wow. I've never seen the night sky like this. Is it always like this here?" Sara, sitting up and gazing to the sky, looked to him and replied with a smile, "It is. Is it not like this in Florida?" Sam replied, "Oh no. There's far too much light pollution around to see it like this." Sara eventually lay down next to Sam and crossed her arms behind her head, as the two looked skyward. Sam felt his heart pick up a few beats of pace as she did, and he asked, "What do your parents do?" Sara replied, "Well, my mother passed away when I was five, so dad and grandpa mostly raised me."

"Oh...I'm sorry to hear that. I didn't mean to bring that up."

"It's okay. I don't have much memory of her, but I do wish she was here. My dad told me she was the best thing to ever happen to him...well, next to me." Sam smiled at the statement as Sara then asked, "And you?"

"Well, both my parents came from Hialeah, which is where I was raised. Dad's a lawyer and mom does childcare. I've got a younger brother, Luiz, who is going into the military when he graduates high school in a couple of years." Sara moved closer to Sam and Sam felt as if the mere touch of her was going to drive him wild. A rush of blood coursed through his neck, as he felt his breathing start to quicken. Sara looked to him and said with a playful tone in her voice, "It's a bit chilly out here, I hope you don't mind warming a girl up."

Sam replied with a smooth bravado as his voice lowered nearly into a growl, "Come get warm then." He said, surprised at the words that just left his mouth as Sara tucked into his chest. He could smell the scent of her hair, fragrant with flowers of some sort. Sam took the smell in and asked Sara, "Is that honey and wildflower?" Sara looked to him, shocked and said, "Actually, yes!" Sam felt a split of emotions, as if his normal insecure self was contesting with some bestial, primal side to him as he felt his nerves relax, and his senses heighten. The scent and touch of her alone was beginning to intoxicate him, and he savoured this moment out in the wild, just the two of them.

Chapter 10: A Hunt in the Dark

Sara said with a breathy tone, "Don't suppose you'd mind if we shared a little more heat?" She playfully grabbed the collar of his shirt as he replied in a collected voice, "It *is* rather chilly out here. Can't let you freeze now, huh?" Sara exhaled a short breath and clawed at his collar as Sam felt the nails graze his skin. The two looked to each other and moved in, Sam's mouth finally meeting Sara's soft lips. The two embraced and felt a mutual wave of affection roll over them, one that had been building since they started talking in the fall. As she held on tighter, the roar of a mountain cat nearby abruptly halted the two.

Both looking around, Sam felt his blood burn again, this time in response to possible danger. Sara, with a tone of worry taking over her voice, said, "Sam, I think we should go." Sam got up and flicked the lantern on, and a light ensconced the two on the rock. As if blessed with a sixth sense, he could almost feel the presence of the large cat. Sam pointed past the car, "It's that way. And coming."

"How can you tell? I can't see a thing beyond the light," Sara asked, straining her eyes to see what Sam did. Sam replied, "I can sense it. Listen closely, you can almost hear it walking this way." Sara listened for a time in the silence but could only hear her heartbeat picking up speed. Sam said to her, "Listen. I'll get down and try to meet it. Maybe I can scare it off. You get in the car and start it, so that way it'll have me to go through, instead of both of us waiting for it.

"Sam, no! You've fought one guy and now you think you can take a mountain lion?" Sara asked, panic rising in her. Sam looked to her and immediately retorted, "I'm not trying to fight it. I'm giving you the chance to get the car ready and keep you safe. Come down after I do and get in."

Sam, his sight adjusting well to the night, slid off the boulder and landed on his feet with the lantern in hand. He helped Sara down a moment later and started walking to the passenger side of the car, awaiting the cat's next move. Sara hurried and got in the car as she heard a roar and a series of steps from it nearby. Sam immediately dodged as a dark missile flew past his ear. A sting of pain caught him in the side as he caught a glimpse of the large mountain cat. The predator turned around to face Sam and stared with glowing yellow eyes, ready to take another leap at the young man.

Sam somehow knew if he made any move to the car, the mountain lion would strike. He decided he was going to have to move, and fast. Sam began to slowly inch back for the door as the mountain lion moved in. Growling, it suddenly sprang into action and jumped for him. Sam held the lantern up and time slowed as he got a much better view of the cat. It had pale yellow fur with spots on it, and two black streaks that ran from its eyes. The cat flinched long enough for Sam to thrust his foot forward in a solid kick, catching the beast in the nose. A growl of pain emanated from it as it lost its posture mid-pounce and slammed into Sam. Both smacked the front wheel well with a *bang* as Sara screamed. Sam got to his feet and smashed the lantern over its head, upon which the fluid and fire splashed. Sam quickly saw that was no mountain lion, but a leopard! The creature howled in agony as flames caught it on the side of its face. Driven by pain and panic, the leopard made a series of swipes, two which batted Sam in the chest and shoulder. He felt his head spin as the warm sensation of something wet began to pool up where he had been hit. Sam reflexively threw his foot back and kicked forward again with all his might, catching the leopard squarely in the ribs. The cat huffed a cough as the wind was driven from it, still trying to put the flames out. Sam threw the door open, crashed into the seat, closed it, and sat back as Sara immediately threw the car into reverse, then cut a semi-circle back before peeling off down the road. The flames on the large cat died out as Sam started to struggle with breathing. Turning on the overhead light, he saw that he was bleeding in three areas. Sara cried out, "Sam! You're hurt! We need to get you to a hospital!" Sam replied, fighting off a wave of pain, "I'll be fine. It didn't get me deep, just some flesh wounds is all." "Flesh wounds, my ass! Your shirt is soaked with blood!" Sam steadied his breathing as a voice in his head gently said, *"Focus on the present. Steady your breathing. You can't heal properly without steady breathing."* Sam was baffled at what he heard yet felt comforted and strangely familiar with the voice. His breathing became deeper, more rhythmic and paced again as his sense returned to him. The open wounds were still burning, but he felt in his right mind again. Sara said, "Please, try to stay conscious. I'll get you to a hospital soon." Sam felt his head getting light again, but his breathing and being were calm as he replied, "I'll be perfectly calm the entire way." Sara, utterly shocked at how composed he was, felt herself relax a bit by his state of being, and continued down the road for a hospital.

Chapter 11: Assessing the Damage

Sam didn't remember falling asleep, only waking up with a bright light shining on him as his vision cleared up. A few figures were standing over him, blurred at first with distant voices. As he roused and regained his senses slowly, his vision focused, and the voices became clearer as he saw masks on faces and dark green scrubs. One with glasses stood over him and said, "Ah, you're awake! How do you feel?" Sam looked and saw he had a saline IV in his arm. His shirt was gone with nothing else left but his wounds, some of which had stitches in them. The doctor said, "You're a resilient one, Mr. Cruz. Despite being half bled out, you managed to walk yourself into the ER until we got you. Get into a fight with a mountain lion, I heard?"
Sam replied, "A leopard, actually." The doctor paused and replied, "Leopard? We don't get those out here. Those are jungle cats." Sam cocked his head, puzzled. Deciding to not further discuss the issue, he said, "Can I leave and go home?" The doctor replied, "Technically, we don't want you leaving due to how close of a call it was with you. But seeing as you have no head or serious injuries beyond some nasty gashes, you should be fine to leave in an hour or so. We'll finish running your paperwork, then you can go.
An hour after the doctor cleared him, Sam walked out into the waiting room where he saw a very worried Sara staring at the windows. Her eyes were red, no doubt from likely crying as he took a seat next to her and teased, "Nice night, huh?" Sara spun her head around to see Sam next to her and immediately threw her arms around him, taking care not to squeeze too tightly.
"Oh my God, Sam, I thought you were going to die!" she choked out, warm tears running down her face. He held her close and replied, "Didn't mean to worry you there. I'll be okay. Doc says I'm a bit roughed up, but fine otherwise." One of the nurses approached the two and smiled at their reunion before saying to Sam, "I'll leave your papers here. I don't know what you're made of, but you heal really quickly." With that, she turned from the two and headed back to the ER side. Sara said to Sam, "Why don't you come stay with me for the night? It's the least I can do after saving me back there." Sam nodded and replied, "I'd very much like that."
An hour later, Sara pulled up to where Sam assumed was her place. It was a cosy cabin, akin to his and Fred's, but larger. The two got out of the car and made their way to the door, where Sara unlocked the latch and opened the door. Stepping inside, she flipped a light that revealed a very tidy living room. Two small

couches sat adjacent to each other, both in a right angle facing the television set. There was a small kitchen, with four rooms on each corner of the cabin. In the hall to the right, a passage led to two of the rooms as well as the bathroom. Sam took off his shoes and said to Sara, "This is a nice place! I'm guessing its bigger because it holds more students?" Sara replied, "Indeed. My roommates are gone for the holidays, so it's just me here."
Sara went to a tea kettle and started boiling some water in it, as Sam sat down with a wince on the couch facing the door. Sara walked over to the linen closet in the hall and pulled out a towel. She put it in the bathroom and said, "Whenever you want to shower, there's a towel in

there for you." Sam replied, "Thank you", as he stretched out to help get rid of some of the stiffness from laying in a hospital bed. The tea kettle went off a few minutes later, as Sara poured their tea and came to the couch. Gratefully taking his glass, the warm aromatic smell of maple wafted into Sam's nostrils. Sara looked up and down his body, assessing the wounds as she said, "I hope those don't scar over too badly. It looks rough."

Sam swallowed his sip and replied, "It's not too bad now. I'm a bit sore, but nothing terrible." Sara leaned into him, resting her head on his arm. Taking his arm to put around her back, she leaned her head on him and said, "Well, I'm glad you're okay." Sam stared at the door, replaying the events in his head. Sam then said to Sara, "That cat was a leopard. What in the world are leopards doing out here?"

Sara looked up at Sam, and replied, "It did have spots, didn't it?" Sam nodded and replied, "Yeah. I thought it a strange sight. The doctor even confirmed it." Sitting in silence again, Sam then asked, "I don't know why, but I've got this feeling that maybe your great-great grandfather would have something on this. What if the legends are true?"

"You mean the tale about how people could turn into animals?"

"Yes. How else would a leopard get here? If you think about it, there's folklore out here about wendigos and Skinwalkers, right? They change forms in their stories. What if this legend is particularly true?" Sara thought on it for a moment, then said, "It wouldn't be a bad idea. My dad wants nothing to do with those tales, but my grandpa always had a fervent reverence for them. Maybe he could tell us something."

"I'm starting to think that the night up on the mountain didn't just happen to be some random spooky happening. I think it may hold more water than we give it credit for."

"That may be so. Let's not think about that too much tonight, though. You tussled with a leopard and lived to tell about it. Why not focus on relaxing with me?" Sara put a hand to his chest, which shot another rush of burning blood through him, easing his nervousness and making him far more comfortable with her touch and presence. Looking at his watch, Sam said, "That's a lovely thought. I'm famished, though: would you like to order a pizza?" Sara looked up with a big smile on her face and said, "Absolutely! I'll treat! Let me go call them really quick." Sara sprung up and scooted off for the kitchen as Sam leaned his head back, smiled and sighed. Despite facing off with a leopard, he'd had a wonderful day with Sara, and was relieved to find that she shared the same attraction he did to her.

The Jaguar King   L. E. Zimmerman
day with Sara, and was relieved to find that she shared the same attraction he did to her.

Chapter 12: Recoup

That very same night, a leopard limped into a mountainside structure and reverted into a human. Bradley slid against a wall and slunk down to the ground. Feeling his face and neck, it still was very tender and raw from the fire of the lantern. Gritting his teeth in pain, he spat, "Dammit Sam, you're tougher than I thought, I'll give you that." Bradley reached into his pocket and took out a salve that Rodrigo had taught him to make. Rubbing some of the balm on his wound, the salve began to help cull some of the residual burn.

Bradley's head reeled with pain as he thought back on the events of the night. He saw the look in Sam's eyes, completely different than before. It was as though he knew who he was, without knowing it was Bradley. He recalled seeing the two on the rock, and a raging pang of jealousy flashing through his mind. All his instincts turned to hunting Sam in that moment as he ruminated on the incident. Rodrigo walked in on the sight of Bradley on the ground and said in a caustic voice, "I told you not to engage him. Yet, here you are, exactly as I warned. I hope you learned."

"I know. I made an error. You were correct," Bradley said sullenly.

Rodrigo sighed and said, "Listen, my protégé, I understand you're eager for the fight. I understand that feeling myself very much. There's a time to bide time and plan, and a time to fight. Knowing the difference is a valuable skill to have."

"You've lived far longer than I have, I should indeed be listening better to your advice."

"Indeed. So now that you learned your lesson, get the rest you can tonight. Tomorrow, we continue your training."

The next day Bradley was following the movements that Rodrigo showed him. A series of blows and counters, blocks, steps and movements from the style he once had, as ruler of his old tribe from centuries ago. Bradley would mimic each move, some with difficulty, some with ease. The knowledge and muscle memory were all starting to come together, as he felt memories of a lifetime back take him over and aid in learning the moves.

Over the next few weeks, Bradley was introduced to and endured rigorous exercise, far beyond the likes he'd ever endured. Baseball conditioning was nothing to what he was subjected to. Rodrigo had him perform rigorous, brutal exercises like carrying boulders from one end of the training space to the other, for time. Other ones included climbing certain routes on the mountain for time. If he

failed to meet the time Rodrigo set, he would be awarded more
work to do.

The first few days he upchucked several times, unaccustomed to
such work. During a run, his lungs burned so intensely that he
thought he was going to drop. Rodrigo would simply encourage
him on in his arduous tasks, be it by word or by force. Whenever
Bradley thought of giving up, Rodrigo reminded him of Sam, and
how he had handed him two humiliations in a

row. The anger and spite would drive Bradley on, and it didn't take long for him to start reaching into the war chief's essence for help, when he was almost at his limits.

As the days passed, Rodrigo took note of his progress and approved of what he saw, but always emphasized there was more to do. One day, Bradley was sparring with Rodrigo and was knocked off his feet. Reaching into his essence, the memory of the war chief came back to aid him, as he caught his fall on the shoulder blades of his back, swung his legs straight over his head and kicked back up immediately. Rodrigo knew of this kip-up from his time, having sparred with his war chief in the past, and quickly countered by sweeping Bradley's feet out from under him, sending him back to the ground.

Looking over the young man, Rodrigo said, "You're growing better, young one. But know this: relying too much on your essence doesn't make you better. You must improve on your own power to gain the ability needed to defeat your adversary."

Bradley sat up and said, "I understand. Can we take a break?" Rodrigo nodded and began to head to the entrance of the chamber. Stopping, he said in a serious tone, "Bradley, I need you to watch the place and train while I'm gone. I'm leaving to find the other essence users and unite them under our banner." Bradley, a look of surprise on his face forming, stood up and replied, "Rodrigo, what about my training?"

"Bradley, I've shown you all you need to know. You simply must do the work to grow better. I know you can."

"How long will you be gone?"

"A few months, I estimate. I need to acclimate to the world. Gods know how much it's changed since I've walked the world."

Bradley digested the weight of what he was being told, then nodded and said, "Very well. Find the other essence users. I'll grow stronger so I can take Sam's away!" Rodrigo looked back to Bradley and smiled, then replied, "I know you will."

Chapter 13: History Unfolded

A week after the fight Sam had with the leopard, his wounds had recovered incredibly quickly, and he'd begun undertaking a workout regimen. Sara would occasionally protest and say he wasn't in any shape to try to be working out, but the night of the attack gave Sam an unprecedented motivation to train heavily, so that no one could ever bring harm to him or Sara, or anyone he cared about again.

Sara could only protest so much, seeing as his wounds did indeed heal amazingly fast, and the notion of him getting stronger to better defend her subtly enamoured her. Every day in the morning, Sam would perform a solid hundred repetitions of sit ups, squats, push-ups, ten pull ups, and go for a mile run. Despite the cold Colorado winter being in full effect, Sam pushed through the brisk chill and would increase his time and recovery amongst the regimen.

Weeks later, the other students and Sigma Pi had all returned from holiday break. Fred and Sam happily reunited, sharing how each one's break went to the other. Upon sharing the night of the incident, Fred replied, "Well damn, dude. You're really coming into your own. You fought off a damn leopard? I bet Sara liked that. No wonder you two are dating now."

Sam laughed and replied, "It's good to see you're back, Fred."

"Are you coming to dinner tonight with the guys?"

"I'm actually going to meet Sara's family tonight, but I'll rain check with you all!"

Fred replied, "No problem, bud. Good to see you're okay. I still don't know how a leopard is in Colorado, but whatever it was, you still whipped its ass."

Later in the evening, Sara and Sam reached her family's house and parked the car. Taking a deep breath, she looked at him and said, "Ready to meet the family?"

Sam smiled with a confident look and replied, "Of course." The two got out and headed to the door, as Sara opened it for the two to walk inside. Looking around, it was a homely arrangement with wood burning in the fireplace. Pictures of the family were hung up on the walls, and beyond the living room stood a large kitchen, as well as a set of stairs that led to the second floor at the door.

Looking around, Sara noticed something and said, "Dad must be gone. His keys are always on the coffee table unless he's out." A voice in the kitchen said with a jolly tone, "Hey now, do I hear my granddaughter?"

An older man walked out, in suspenders, jeans and a green sweater. His hair was silver, which matched the wrinkles on his face. His posture and bright green eyes, however, showed little signs of any aging, as he briskly made his way for the two. "Grandpa!" Sara cried as she ran for the older man and hugged him. After doing so, she turned to Sam, she smiled and said, "This is Sam, my boyfriend. He came to college here from Florida. He's the one that saved me when we were out and about that night." The man looked at Sam up and down, appraised him, then approached him with a smile and outstretched arm. He said happily, "Hey, Sam! I'm Edward DuMont, Sara's grandpa! You can call me Ed!" Sam eagerly shook Ed's hand, and felt a firm grasp of latent strength that clearly belied the old man's stature. "Pleasure to meet you!" Sam replied with a wide smile, already taking a liking to Ed. Ed said to the two, "Come on to the kitchen, I'll put in some coffee and deer steak!" Sam looked to Sara with excitement and the three headed there. Ed started up the coffee brewer and turned on the stove, as the other two sat down at the table. Slicing a small cut of butter and throwing it into the pan, Ed then took some cuts of deer meat out of the fridge and put them on the pan, upon which the meat then hissed as it met the metal. Pouring the two each a mug of coffee, Sam and Sara gratefully accepted their drinks as Ed took one for himself and sat down. Taking a sip of the drink, Ed grinned and asked, "So, how did you two become a thing?"

Sara uneasily replied, "Well, Sam and I have been talking since we met at SRV Steakhouse. The night we became official, we were attacked by a large cat." Ed grimaced at the mention and said, "Goodness, glad to see you both all right." Sara paused for a moment then replied, "That's the thing. We're not sure if everything is okay." Ed stared for a moment before Sara continued, "Look, we believe that the old legends may not just be old legends." Sam took a sip, then with a serious look on face, explained, "I was on Mount Elbert for a Sigma Pi initiation, and long story short, our frat president said some weird chant that ended up bring about some light that knocked us all out. I don't know why, but I've got this strange feeling that we woke up something. The cat that attacked us wasn't just some mountain lion, it was a leopard."

Ed's face had a shadow fall over it, his expression turned grim. Setting his coffee down, Sara asked, Grandpa, is everything okay?" Ed checked the meat and flipped it, then sat back down. He slowly said to the two, "Look, what I'm about to say, you may not believe. But there's a legend that's been passed in my family that started with my own grandfather.

"There's a tale that back in the day, there was a group of shapeshifters that could turn into leopards. I know it sounds weird, but there's more to it. A group of humans and these draconic beings called wyverns sealed them with some magic talisman, then purportedly buried it here. Some believe a wyvern was the last guardian of the seal, and brought it here, far from the shapeshifters for safe keeping." Looking to an unnerved Sam, Ed asked, "Do you remember the chant?"

"Not off the top of my head, no." Sam paused after his response and started to hear a faint voice in his head, whispering the chant. Ed looked at the young man's unease upon getting lost in thought and his suspicions only grew as Sam focused in on what he was hearing. "There's something about...from blood, to man, to beast and back again. At least, what it translates to." After a minute, the chanting stopped. Ed beckoned for Sam to follow him. Both him and Sara followed Ed as he led them to the basement door. Opening it, Ed led the two downstairs. Sara looked around and asked, "Grandpa, is there something down here you haven't told me?" Ed looked back to her and responded, "My dear granddaughter, what's down here is stuff your dad never wanted to talk about with you. But I fear it may be time to have that talk." Making his way to an old metal cabinet, Ed pulled out a key from his pocket and inserted it into the lock at the handle, before turning it. A clicking sound was heard and Ed pulled down on the handle, swinging the door open. He scanned the upper shelf and to the left, found an old book looking like it had seen more than a century of existence.

Opening it, Ed began to read intently the contents of its pages, while Sam and Sara looked at each other, then to Ed, breaths bated as to what he could be reading. Sara glanced to Ed and asked, "Grandpa...what is it?" Ed licked his forefinger as he flipped through the pages. He then found a spot, put the finger in between the pages and handed the book to Sam. Nodding to him, he said, "Sam, I think you should read this."

Looking to the page Ed left open for him, Sam's eyes grew wide as he read the page.

"This...this is the chant. Not only that...but it describes the same kind of light and experience I had on the mountain that night." Ed crossed his arms and asked, "I bet from that night, your senses have been heightened, you're more alert, more capable, and feel as though someone else lives in your head, right?"

"Yeah! How do you know?!"

"Sam, my own grandfather was around when all of this stuff first happened long ago."

"What do you mean, around?" Sara asked. Ed looked to her and replied, "Your great-great grandfather, Edis DuMont was part of an old secret society order formed to take on and stop them."

Chapter 14: A Family Line

"Great-great grandpa Edis?" Sara asked, the name strangely ringing a bell with Sam. Ed nodded and responded, "Back in the 1800s, a group called the Jan Damis were around. They were leopard shapeshifters that pulled a lot of strings then. Grandpa Edis was part of the order called the Dracosapiens that stopped them. Now, there's lots more detail in the book that can explain it better than I ever will, but Mount Elbert is a resting place for a great wyvern, as well as the seal that put the Jan Damis away, according to Edis's book."

Sam read through the pages and found a section on the shapeshifters and essences, as he exclaimed, "All of this...I've been experiencing this!!! It reads that shifters who bear the essence gain the abilities of a leopard, as well as sometimes the access to the former user's knowledge base if they were a strong soul." Sara looked to Sam and added, "That may explain the leopard we saw that night, as well as how you were able to fend it off so readily." Ed looked to Sam and said, "So it's true...you saw a leopard out there. That very likely means they're back. And you may have one of the essences in you." Sam looked to Ed and said, "The night I was on Mount Elbert, the chant was done around a massive bone of sorts. The light was a bright yellow, much like described in the book. Since then, all of these things have come to light. Ed, was Edis a shifter as well?"

Ed shook his head and replied, "No. He did make mention in the book that one of his friends took the essence of a Jan Damis and went undercover as a spy in their ranks during the Jan Damis hunt. The campaign against them went for decades, and he was one of the top researchers for the team."

"Grandpa, did I hear you say wyvern? As in a *dragon?!*" Sara asked, emphasizing the dragon part. Ed nodded and replied, "Oh yeah, you heard right, sweetheart. Dragons were apparently real then, as well. They teamed up with the humans, for they were the mortal enemy of the shifters. I'm not sure if any are alive by now, sounds like they were hunted to extinction. Whichever ones survived, didn't have enough to carry on the line. Mount Elbert is a resting place for the leader of the wyverns, as well as one of the two generals of the Dracosapiens. Illixus, I believe his name was."

"Well grandpa, this is certainly a lot to process," Sara said, letting the details settle in her mind. Sam kept reading through the book and said, "There's no doubt by this point that I have the essence of a shifter."

Ed looked to Sam and said, "There's a high chance you do. Have you shifted yet?" Sam shook his head and replied, "Not yet. I've tapped into the abilities of the leopard, and whoever had this essence before, but not the leopard itself yet." Ed looked to Sam and replied, "Well, I'd say it'd be a good time to learn. If there's others out there, and they're freed, I worry things may not be so kind in upcoming days."

"Can't we call the police?" Sara asked. Ed gently replied to her, "It's the smart thing a person would do, yes. However, the police are neither going to believe a story of being assaulted by shapeshifting humans, nor would it warrant their concern. We'd need evidence and it sounds like beyond this book, we've nothing to give them. We're on our own with this." Sam looked to Ed with great concern on his face and asked, "Ed, how many Jan Damis existed back then?"

"There were thousands of them. It took a whole order of wyverns and humans to stop them." Sam's eyes grew wider as he asked, "Do you think there's that many out there now?"

Ed replied, "I'm not sure how many there are now, but the book says that originally the essences were all fragments of five greater ones. Hopefully, they aren't fragmented and whole again. Best case scenario, we'd at least know there's a reasonable number."

Sara said with a quiver in her voice, "That means there's still that one leopard out there that attacked us. Which means it wasn't just a leopard, but a human." Sam added, "Maybe this was the essence talking, but I felt like it was a familiar essence I knew. Probably whoever used this in their past life knows the other."

Ed said, "Sam, I do have an artefact from my grandfather that may help commune with whoever had that essence before." Reaching up into the cabinet, he pulled out a stone spike, finely smoothed down with etchings on it. He handed it to Sam and said, "Here. When you're alone, take this and meditate with it. It's a finding from the temple which the seal was from as well. This apparently helped shifters commune better with other users throughout the line. It may help, if the book holds true to what may be happening."

Sam took the spike and felt a wave of familiarity hit him as the voice returned in his head. It whispered something, then went silent as he pocketed the spike.

"Thank you, Ed" Sam said, before looking to Sara. "Listen, I'm going to my place to meditate with this thing. I need answers and fast, especially if all of this is true." Sara went up to Sam and hugged him, then said, "I understand. Do what you must. Please call me if anything comes up." Ed walked up to Sam and clapped him on the shoulder, then said, "You're welcome to use the book too, if you must. I know this wasn't the best first meeting of the family, but I promise it was great to meet you!" Sam laughed at Ed's remark, feeling his mood lighten.

"Thanks Ed. I don't mean to leave so soon, but I've got the feeling this stuff is coming back to light, and this book only proves it. I know most sane people would immediately disregard such tales, but if this was passed down in your family for generations and describes exactly what I've been experiencing of late, there's more than coincidence here happening."

Chapter 15: Connecting with the Past

Later that day, Sam returned to his room and waited for Fred to go on an evening date with a girl he had been talking to, before pulling out the spike. Sam held on to the spike and sat down in the middle of the floor. Taking a deep breath, he closed his eyes and began to focus on the artefact.

"Great spirit, or whoever is out there: if you can hear me, please come to me." Silence hung in the air and Sam felt nothing. Opening one of his eyes, the room still looked as it was, with no changes. Closing it, he began to focus harder. "Please, if you're in there, come to me. I have lots of questions that need answering." A subtle shift in the air was felt and Sam felt his head growing dizzy, much like the night on the mountain. Unsettled, Sam opened his eyes and saw the lights starting to get pulled out of the room. The whispers returned and began to grow louder, rising to a crescendo, until silence returned with much of the light gone. A humanoid figure in blue light appeared before him and sat across from him. Sam, bewildered, scanned the being from top to bottom. He could see through him like a thin sheet, yet he had discernible features. He wore a pelt of leopard skin, with long smooth hair that ran down to his back. A headband was worn across his forehead, and his figure was quite powerful. His dense musculature was accentuated by his broad chin and thick neck. The man spoke in an eerie voice with a faint echo, "At last, a worthy successor."

"Me?" Sam asked, highly uneasy at what he was looking at.

"Yes, you, Sam," the man replied, his voice strangely calm, yet faintly resonating with latent power. "Since joining with you, I've watched everything you do, and know you're worthy."

"But why? I'm the last person to be...whatever you are or were."

"I am the iron shaman, Hanska, of the Parduska tribe. My path was one walked of peace and fury."

Sam couldn't believe his eyes: he was talking to the essence of some tribe member from long ago that held his essence.

"Hanska...I see. You already know who I am, yes?"

"I do. I share a body with you now. I'm one of the essences that can speak directly to you. All essences have the capability to in some way, shape or form, but I can manifest before you with enough connection."

"Through meditation?"

"Yes. I see the spirit stake is in your possession now as well. It grants the holder the ability to connect with the essence plane."

"The essence plane?"

"The plane where essences exist. Essences are not souls, so much as they are remnants of the person's energy and being in a manifested form. Both my body and spirit passed long ago. However, the part of me bonded to the leopard remains, as it does with all other essences."

"I see. So...what led you to choosing me as your successor, let alone even finding me?"

Hanska looked Sam in the eyes and brought the vision of the mountain back, where the event replayed in slow motion.

"When the essences were unsealed, there were a total of six of us. The Leopard King, Rodrigo was the head of our tribe. From what I can gather, he may still walk the earth yet. As all the essences were unsealed that night, I felt a connection to you from the incantation. When we were released, I saw that you defended your friend and had a good head on your shoulders. Once I found my way to you, I saw some of your memories and learned you were timid, yet kind. I wanted to help strengthen you."

Sam looked at the vision as a light flew into his body on the mountain, passing out not along after. He then saw a man swathed in robes take Bradley off the mountain while he was unconscious.

"Strengthen me? I guess I appreciate it. It's still a lot for me to take in," Sam said, running a hand over the scars from the fight with the leopard.

"Ah yes, your wounds from the fight with your friend."

"My friend?" Sam asked, a curious eyebrow raised.

"You saw in the vision that your friend Bradley was taken, yes?"

"Wouldn't call him much of a friend after that night, but sure."

"Look harder." Sam focused his attention to the vision as Bradley was carried off. The vision blew away like fog on the ground from a gust, as it showed the night of the leopard attack. Sam felt the ping of familiarity again and with Hanska's help, saw a spirit form over the leopard. It was Bradley.

"You mean THAT was Bradley?!" Sam asked, perplexed by the revelation.

"Yes."

"But...why? I thought he left the college?"

"I have suspicions that he may be taking orders from Rodrigo, if he indeed walks again."

"Who is Rodrigo?"

"Rodrigo is an essence holder with the unique ability to let himself manifest physically. So long as he does not catch a fatal disease or is murdered, his lifespan extends abnormally long. It's how he survived into later years." Hanska switched the vision to one of his

own memories. As Sam watched through Hanska's eyes, he caught
a glimpse of the robed man again. Hanska was

running after Rodrigo, and chased him into a temple where a woman was laid on an altar within. Rodrigo stopped and said to Hanska, "Don't you see? She's the living relative of the progenitor! With her sacrifice, we can obtain the power of the leopard shifters for ourselves!"

Hanska cried back to him, drawing a dagger, "Rodrigo, don't do this! I will cut you down if I must!" Rodrigo smiled, drew his own and drove it into the chest of the woman. Her eyes went wide as she struggled to get any sound out of her throat. Blood began to pool up and run down her sides as Hanska cried in agony. Sam felt a burning rage unlike any other well up within him, no doubt feeling as Hanska did that night. Hanska dashed for Rodrigo and nearly brought the dagger home, only for a blinding light to knock him off his feet.

A woman's voice gently said to him in the darkness, "Do not worry, my beloved. For even though I'm gone from this world, the six parts of me will live on. You have my memories and my will, which will give you the power you need to take on Rodrigo. Until we meet again."

Sam felt his stomach start to knot up, the intense sorrow of her passing carrying over to him as well. The vision faded away as Hanska reappeared and said, "That night, my love Marcela was slaughtered because of Rodrigo. Whereas once I faithfully served him, that had all turned to hatred. Rodrigo escaped that night from me and went into hiding. Though I searched for him all my life, I could not find him and eventually grew old and passed. Now, I suspect he walks again, and needs to be stopped."

Sam took a deep breath, sorting out all that he had just seen. He then said, "Well, Hanska, this is quite a bit for me to handle. I simply wanted to join a college fraternity, not inherit some centuries-old power from a tribe."

"I understand it is indeed quite a bit for you to process. And if you so choose to be rid of this, I hold the incantation in my memories that lets you free yourself from me." Sam sat upon the option for a time, then thought of the leopard, no, Bradley's attack that night. He thought of how scared Sara was, and that he'd do anything to protect her. He thought of the night on the mountain, and thought of how he saved Fred.

"Hanska," Sam said, his voice growing steady. "I don't want to be rid of this. At least not yet. I've got too many I care for that could be hurt. If I don't learn to use this, they may suffer because of it. Please, teach me all that you know." Hanska nodded and replied,

"Very well. Find somewhere secluded. Let us begin. I've a feeling Bradley and or Rodrigo will be back for vengeance."

Chapter 16: The Way of the Iron Shaman

Sam drove to a small woodland area he knew, not far from his place and parked his car. Upon exit, he followed the blue figure of Hanska into the woods for a time, before they arrived at a clearing. Hanska turned to Sam and said, "First, we'll begin with your battle reflexes. I was one of two top warriors of my tribe and prided myself on combat ability. Fortunately, you get to benefit from having immediate access to all I know, and have displayed good usage of it time and time again." Hanska rushed Sam suddenly and threw a series of punches, all of which Sam immediately dodged on instinct and weaved through, before countering with one of his own. His fist wisped through Hanska who turned to Sam and smiled.

"Exactly what I mean. Now, do not solely rely on my own prowess to get you through battles. Time has passed and the opponents for which I've fought in my time are not the same as the ones you have and will fight. You must also learn to grow your own ability, train yourself, enhance your mind, spirit and body for such things." Sam looked at his fist, unclenched it, looked to Hanska and replied, "I've already started working out. Does that help?"

"Yes. A wise choice from your last encounter. The stronger you become, the better my ability will lend itself to you. You can also grow your own ability with mine added to it. I'm long since deceased, so my knowledge has limits. But you? You're alive, still learning, still adapting. Your life can take what I've learned and expand it tenfold over."

Sam nodded, and smiled at knowing that having the latent skill of Hanska within him would help build his own.

"All right. What's next?"

"You must gain mental fortitude. I know you're easily unsettled by most things that make you uncomfortable. This I cannot lend, for it is a state of being versus a knowledge your body can recreate. You must develop your own."

"Any methods of doing that?" Sam asked. Hanska lifted his arms up as his figure split off into duplicates. Sam raised his fists in the style he saw Hanska do from the memories, his left arm across his sternum and his right held close to his chin in a half guard. Hanska attacked from multiple angles as Sam tried his best to defend against them all. He could dodge two of them before the third made contact. Hit by Hanska's foot, Sam felt a wave of pain course from the blow.

"You're an essence! How can you hurt me?" Sam asked, punching through another mirage.

"You're not actually wounded, not physically anyways. You're suffering the mental duress of my assault, and the pain receptors in your brain are tricked into thinking you're feeling the blows. We are linked, after all."

Sam felt his senses spike, completely on edge now that he learned
that Hanska, contrary to his belief prior, could hurt him. Sam was
getting nervous and felt immense pressure as he looked all around
him. Hanska said to him, "You feel cornered, stressed, like your
life is in danger?"
"Of course, I do! It feels like it is!" Sam replied, taking two more
blows from another two duplicates.
Hanska called to him and said, "You must endure! Calm your
nerves, focus on what's at hand. Stay in your thinking mind and
battle back!" Sam took a deep breath, calmed himself down, then
assessed the situation at hand. They were only attacking two at a
time and using pack tactics to open for a follow up hit thus far.
Sam braced up as two duplicates ran at him. He dodged and
countered both. Surely, as he predicted, a third came in to rush
and Sam met it with a kick. The copy dissipated as two more
surprised him.
Sam jumped back and weaved through them, striking each one.
Three more ran to him and overwhelmed him as Sam felt multiple
blows connect, dropping him to the ground. The duplicates all
dissipated as Hanska stood as the only one again before him. Sam
got up and was still trying to work on how he could feel pain, only
to find no lasting injuries shortly after. Hanska nodded and said,
"Well done. Through that, you got the basics of mental fortitude in
action. Enduring the stress led you to adapt and counter.
Remember that feeling and carry it with you in the future."
Sam nodded as he said to Hanska, "Thank you for teaching me all
of this. I guess if this Rodrigo guy is out there, our lives are in
danger, right? Hanska nodded and replied, "His hunger for power
knows no bounds. I'm very glad to assist you. Should you want to
continue this path, you too will earn the title of iron shaman. A
man as ready for peace and understanding as he is for combat."
Sam smiled and replied, "Iron shaman. That's got a nice ring to it."

Chapter 17: An Inevitable Clash

The winter passed into springtime, and the students were all getting anxious for their next break, even as Fred held a pair of sparring mitts for Sam to hit. Through the last three months, Sam had been increasing his training regimen, determined to make himself better able to defend those he cared for. Fred was completely astounded, but completely understood. He watched Sam become someone different than he had known growing up. Here he was, laying expert punches on hitting mitts, each blow finding the mark with incredible precision. Sam had put on a bit of lean muscle from his time training since the incident. He looked more serious, surer of himself, more confident. Fred smiled at the thought that his friend was becoming a greater version of himself as Sam drilled home a straight right into the mitt, before catching his breath.

"Dude, that was pretty intense. You've become quite the beast of late," Fred noted, taking the mitts off his hands. Sam nodded in between breaths and replied, "Thanks. I've been working up to take on that Rodrigo guy for a reason. No way in hell him, his people or anyone is going to threaten you all while I'm around."

"Sigma Pi is down with helping you too. Luckily for you, Donte used to box and has showed you some of what he knows."

"Most certainly. I know this sounds silly, but it's just a feeling I have that at some point, we're gonna run into our leopard friend again." Fred looked at Sam's face and said, "It does. But from what you've shown me, I don't doubt it." The two began packing up the gloves and mitts, and got in Fred's jeep to head back to the Sigma Pi house.

Once they arrived there, the two got out as Donte approached them on the steps. Fred said to Donte, "What's up, Donte?" Donte, with a serious look on his face said to the two, "It's a letter for Sam. Not sure exactly who sent it." Sam felt a twinge of unease creep into his being as he took the letter and opened it. There wasn't a return address or a large body to the letter. It simply read:

"WE'LL HAVE OUR REMATCH YET. BE READY, PLEDGE."

"What does it say?" Steve asked, approaching the others.

"It means Bradley is coming for me. As well as that Rodrigo guy, most likely," Sam replied, a tone of anger welling up in him. Donte laughed and said, "Man, you took his ass last time no problem. You got this. I know you both are magical now, or whatever the hell is going on with you. But we believe in you."

Sam looked to Donte and replied, "Thank you. I hope I'll be ready for him. I guess it's real now that I've seen it in writing."

Steve asked, "When do you think he'll come after you? You know, after the last time he came after you and Sara?"

"Honestly, I'm not sure. I've been getting used to having the ability myself, and still have a bit of trouble switching into the leopard form. But from the way that letter reads, it won't be long."

"Dude, I couldn't believe my eyes when I first saw you do that! That was insane!" Steve exclaimed, motioning with his hands, the movements of a leopard. Sam smiled and replied, "Yeah, it's something else. Now if he comes for any of you as well, please don't take him yourself. I'll deal with him."

"A wise person would open fire and start shooting his ass, but how do you tell the cops that you shot a guy who can turn into a leopard?" Donte said, bringing a few laughs from the fraternity about. Sam laughed and then replied, "Honestly, I don't want to kill the guy. I just want to stop him and let him think about attacking us while he's in jail."

Fred looked to Sam, clapped a hand on his shoulder and said, "No matter what, we're here for you. We won't go after him, but that doesn't mean we're going to let him just walk in the door if he comes. A group of Sigma Pi fellas and I have your back, pal."

Sam said to the group, "I appreciate it, you guys. I'm sorry that you all got caught up in this centuries-old ordeal. I'm going to see Sara for a bit, so whatever you do, don't get into too much trouble now, okay?"

The guys all laughed as Sam started walking to his car that he had left at the frat house earlier, got in and took off. Upon turning on to the road, Sam sighed and mentally called for Hanska. Hanska appeared in the seat next to him and said, "You're uneasy. You sense the coming of the other users, yes?"

"I do. It feels as though there's another presence in the mountains that grew bigger, more solid, maybe even more powerful."

"I understand. Most likely Rodrigo. The essence is too familiar for it to be anyone else. He has returned."

"Why hasn't he made a move yet?"

"Rodrigo is powerful, and patient. He does not plan short-sightedly. He must likely be gathering and biding his time."

"I see." Sam clenched tighter on the wheel and tried to focus on the road and the grey overcast daylight sky, to help calm his nerves. "I suppose they want to make their move sooner than we thought. Say...you don't think that Bradley would...you know..."

"Kill you?" Hanska finished for Sam.

"Yeah. That."

"It would be wise to take the precaution that he has every intent to kill you. Take no chances in combat."

"Right, yeah. No chances."

"Sam, that doesn't mean you have to kill him in return. But be prepared that he might not show you the same mercy." Sam continued focusing on the road and before he knew it, the DuMont house came into sight. An ambulance was parked outside with flashing lights as a few paramedics ran inside. A knot formed in Sam's stomach, knowing that the situation was nothing good. Parking the car, he got out and slammed the door before heading around the other side to get in, in order to not interfere with the paramedics. Upon entering the back door, there was a tear-streaked Sara leaning on Ed, with a grandfatherly arm around her, consoling her. The paramedics headed back to the ambulance as Sam entered and asked, "What happened?"

Sara looked up, and the sight of Sam gave her some comfort as she got up and ran to him, throwing herself into his arms. Looking around the room, pictures were knocked off the walls and furniture was damaged as Sara choked out, "Dad...h-he was attacked...and now is heading to ICU."

Sam's eyes lit with shock, and as he looked closer at the walls, he had an idea of what could have done it. There were slash marks on multiple places of the walls, as well as a few bullet holes. Ed looked to Sam and said in a gruff voice, "They came for my son. They know we know they're here."

Sam felt himself go slack and calm, the undercurrent of anger overriding any panic as he replied, "I'll take them down." Hanska said to Sam in his head, *These claw marks aren't from your friend. This is from Rodrigo. The claw marks are much bigger.* Sam took note of the info as he sat with Sara.

"Sam...please be careful...I don't want anything to happen to you too," Sara managed to say. Running a hand down her long red hair, Sam replied, "I will. I'll go and handle them."

Sam stayed with Sara at the DuMont house for the rest of the evening and felt his senses rise to stay on high alert. While he sensed nothing out of the ordinary, the threat was much closer than he anticipated and he knew he would have to make a move soon, or risk losing more. For the night, he stayed by Sara's side while Ed kept some of his firearms ready, in case any more of them were to show.

By nightfall, both were in Sara's room, with Sam lying next to her on her bed as she said, "Sam, I'm sorry you got dragged into all of this. You just wanted to get a degree coming all the way from

Florida." Sam smiled and replied, "Don't be. I'm sorry that I was partly responsible for bringing this mess about. Listen, we're going to be okay. I've gotta take the fight to them, and soon. The longer I wait, the more danger everyone gets in."

"You don't have to do this alone, you know that, right?"

"I have to take the two on myself. Physically, I'm the only one capable. Knowing the Sigma Pi guys, a few will want to tag along to make sure I'll be okay. I promise I won't be completely alone, though."

"Good. I don't need you back in the hospital too, or worse. I want you here, with me and grandpa." With that, she kissed him and nuzzled her head into his chest. Sam looked out of the window into the night and felt a little more at ease being next to Sara.

Chapter 18: Timeless Leopard

"Finally, the last day!" Bradley exclaimed as he took a sip of wine. Rodrigo smiled and calmly replied, "Yes indeed, my war chief. We've waited long enough. Tomorrow will be a full moon, in which we can take someone to sacrifice, and help us perform the location spell to find the others."

"The location spell?"

"Yes. The Oro Luna is indeed a powerful tool for locating other essence users at a close range. However, across distances, it is useless. There is a spell from my tribe which once someone is sacrificed, their life and blood can be used as a focus point for a locator spell."

Bradley swallowed a gulp of his wine hard, realizing that Rodrigo was intent on making the spell happen. Since the winter, Rodrigo had been gone, traveling around the country, getting used to modern society and catching up on all that he missed. Putting his goblet down, Bradley said, "Leave Sam and Sara be. I'll handle them."

"Oh? I knew you wanted Sam but Sara too?"

"I intend to have her back once I handle Sam."

"I see," Rodrigo nodded with a smile on his face. "Spoken like a true conqueror."

"How did the attack on the DuMont house go?"

"I managed to take down one of them, though he brandished a gun and managed to graze me." Rodrigo held up his arm where the line of a wound ran across and up the shoulder. "He is a good shot; I'll give him that."

"Lucky he didn't hit you directly. Guns are much more powerful than they used to be in your time."

"Back in my own time, we didn't have guns. Just spears, knives, swords, bows and arrows."

"That's true. What's our plan for tomorrow?"

"I'll go and seek out a sacrifice. Likely one of your old former peers. I'll bring them back here, which should likely bait Sam into arriving here as well."

Bradley thought about the last encounter with Sam and was certain that this time he'd get him for sure. Clenching a fist, he said, "Sam won't get lucky this time around. I'll be sure to finish what he started that night."

Rodrigo said, "I've no doubt. Have you been training as I instructed while I was away?" Bradley thought of the constant

hiking and running he had been doing and replied, "Yes. My route
time is incredible now."

"And your mental and spiritual training?"

"I don't need to. The form of the leopard is enough to handle Sam." Rodrigo felt a flash of anger at Bradley's lack of reverence for the other parts of his training, but decided that ultimately, time would tell who would come out on top. Smiling, he said, "For your sake, you had best hope that is indeed all you'll need."

"I think I'll be fine. As for your sacrifice? Sigma Pi house would be your best area to hit. Lots of people to choose from." Rodrigo looked at Bradley, impressed that he so readily recommended the area.

"I see. I will take your recommendation. Now, are you prepared to make the move?"

"I am. Tomorrow by evening, we strike."

"Very good. I will leave you to guard the Oro Luna here and watch the place until I get back. My travels around the world the last couple of months have led me to old texts and scrolls that need to be safeguarded here."

"Then tomorrow it is. I'm excited to find the other users as well."

Chapter 19: The Hunt Begins

Sam was watching the sun go down through the window at his desk, as he finished up an assignment from class. The wind was gently blowing fresh spring air into the room, and he savoured the scent, deeply breathing it in. While finishing up his assignment, he took another look at the sun going down in the mountains. It was a beautiful sight, one that gave him peace and comfort. As he put the assignment in one of his binders, the heavy pull of a presence gave him cause for alarm. Hanska appeared next to him and said with a grim tone, "They're back. Not here, but definitely down here."
Sam got up and ran to the living room. Picking up the phone, he dialled in a number and waited. A voice picked up on the other line.
"Sigma Pi house. This is Donte."
"It's Sam. You may have a guest or two on the way. Get ready."
"Oh, hell yes. Let's whip some ass. You go for the mountain; we'll hold down the fort here."
"Okay. Be safe, guys."
Sam hung up, put on his jacket and headed out the door. Making his way to the car, he got in, started it and headed off for Mount Elbert.
At Sigma Pi house, the sun had set as Donte and the others around the frat house sat waiting for any signs of an intruder or giant cat. Steve held his handgun by his side. The others posted up around various parts of the house with various melee weapons, all ready for someone to come in and start some trouble.
The house was quiet. Silence hung in the air as they all waited on edge for something or someone arrive. Donte clenched his fists and shook his arms around, ready to throw fists with an intruder. The collective air had been tensing the last few days, ever since Sam told them he expected trouble. Normally, any sane human wouldn't believe such things. But when Sam showed them all what he could do, Hanska, the book, the spike and the scars, they were convinced.
As Donte went to look out at a moving shadow from the front window, the lights suddenly cut out. The group all took breaths, doing their best to maintain silence as Steve asked, "The bill for the month was paid, right?"
"Yeah. I don't think this has to do with the bill," Donte replied quietly. He motioned to Steve to follow him outside and Steve moved to his position as the two quietly stepped outside. Moving

around to the back, they went to inspect the breaker and saw the
line had been cut. The

wires were sparking, with the shielding around the cable destroyed. As Donte looked to Steve, glass shattered around the front as several voices were heard screaming. Donte and Steve ran back, flashlights out and pointing to the house. On the porch, the window left of the door was shattered inwards. Donte and Steve jumped in through the window frame and saw something spotted and moving, pouncing around and tackling the Sigma Pi members. Three were already laid out, motionless and another was taken down as well.

"Son of a bitch! Come here!" Donte cried as he ran for the large leopard. The leopard saw him approaching and jumped for him. Donte ducked under its flying body and drove an uppercut home into its ribs. The leopard awkwardly caught itself and rolled behind the couch as Steve drew his gun.

Making sure the leopard wasn't near any of his fraternity brothers, Steve aimed, loaded a magazine in the grip, slid the slide back and aimed with expert dexterity. The leopard's tail flicked from behind the couch and Steve aimed to where he thought the body would be hidden from and shot. A loud bang went off as the muzzle flashed. The cry of a large cat sounded from behind it as all went silent. The remaining members still on their feet tended to the others that were injured, as Steve slowly approached the couch. Turning the corner, he pointed the gun to a spot that had no leopard and his eyes went wide, wondering where it went. No signs of blood were found, either.

As he began to look around, a blur of mass hit him from behind, knocking him to the ground. The leopard snatched his shooting hand with a pair of powerful jaws and tore violently from side to side. Blood went on the walls and floor as Steve screamed in agony, dropping the firearm. The leopard swatted two powerful paws that smashed Steve's head into the floor, leaving him motionless and bleeding. Donte roared with anger as he ran to Steve and began kicking as hard as he could at the leopard's ribs. The giant cat darted away, and Donte followed it, fear overridden by fury at what just happened to his friend.

The leopard abruptly turned around in its path and pounced at Donte. Donte slipped by one of its claws and countered with a left hook, knocking it out through the front door. The leopard spun around as Donte approached and tackled hard, this time hitting him in the stomach. The two went sailing off the porch and into the grass as Donte rolled out the impact, lessening the blow. Popping up to his feet, he and leopard circled one another, each staring each other down. The leopard suddenly said in a human voice, "You must be Donte, the one I was warned about. I must say, you've got great reflexes for a human."

Donte's eyes went wide, perplexed at the fact that the cat spoke to him. He remembered what Sam had told him and replied,

"Thanks. Years of boxing as a Golden Gloves champ are to thank for that. You must be that Rodrigo guy. Pleased to meet you, jackass."

"Indeed. You'd be a fine candidate for sacrifice. What do you say to coming willingly, spare anymore hurt on your comrades, and we'll have no more need to fight?"

"Come get me, pussy cat."

Rodrigo obliged and dashed for Donte as Donte backed up and kicked out at the large cat. His kick missed, and the leopard snagged his leg and brought him to the ground. Donte moved in close and brought Rodrigo into a bear hug, restraining his movements. Donte looked to the porch and saw a dazed Steve staggering out, gun in hand, approaching the two and shouted to him, "Steve! Shoot this damn thing!"
"I don't want the round to potentially hit you, though!"
"Dammit, I said SHOOT HIM!" Steve moved up closer to the two as Rodrigo was tearing at Donte's side with his hind legs, shredding his shirt and drawing blood. Donte positioned his feet under the cat's belly and with a mighty push of desperation, kicked upwards. Rodrigo went up as a shot went off. A howl of pain from Rodrigo sounded as he rolled off and took off into the night, finally giving retreat. A splatter of blood was painted on the grass as Donte laid out on his back, outstretched and catching his breath.
"Donte, are you all right?" Steve asked, going to his friend. Donte sat up and with a grimace of pain, replied, "He hit me good off the porch and tore into my side pretty deep, but I'll live. Probably going to need some damn stitches," Donte replied as he got to his feet. The two headed back inside of the house and Steve stood watch while Donte went to check the status of the others."
A couple of hours had passed, and Sam was at the foot of Mount Elbert, and parked his car near the trail entrance. Shifting into his leopard form, he began his ascent up the trail at triple the speed it would have taken to walk before. The trail had the scent of another, no doubt either Rodrigo or Bradley, and his legs pumped on, making incredible time. Sam was still new to shifting but had been training for the moment.
The night was no problem for him, as his feline night vision kicked in, aiding him clear sight in the dark. His climb took no more than an hour or so. When he reached the top, Sam walked by the spot where the entire ordeal first began. Situated there was the dragon bone of the old wyvern, Illixus. Hanska appeared beside him and said, "Just around the other side and in through a crevasse in the mountain. There's one inside. I can sense him." Sam took note and followed Hanska's directions to a small opening in a pair of boulders. Squeezing through, he made his way inside.

Chapter 20: Rematch

Sam walked through the halls that seemed to have been ornately carved out, etched and expertly made by craftsmen of ages past. Hanska said to him, "This is one of the old hideouts of the Dracosapiens. Be on your guard, for anything could happen."
Now out of his leopard form, Sam had to rely on Hanska to help guide him through the old hideout. Sam said to Hanska, "What did you do in the time of the Jan Damis?"
"I wasn't exactly present for the time of the Jan Damis. When I passed away, Rodrigo sealed my essence within the Oro Luna. I've been dormant within the seal for roughly a millennium or so."
"You mean he didn't utilize you like the others?"
"No. He feared that my ability to easily commune with a user would lead to his downfall. He knew I detested him for what he did in our tribe."
"I see. Well, he's in trouble now that I'm here." Hanska chuckled and replied, "I'm glad that you're here to walk this path, Sam."
The two passed through a long passageway from the selection of halls that led into a wide atrium-like room of sorts. Sam looked ahead and saw the unmistakable form of Bradley, sitting in a chair and drinking a glass of wine. Finishing the glass, he looked to Sam with a smile and stood up.
"Sam Cruz! It's good to see you again. I guess you found the place okay," Bradley taunted, haughtily throwing his glass behind him, and shattering it in the process. Sam replied, "Didn't know you drank wine. I recall you drinking cheap beer."
"My tastes have become refined with my...awakening."
"You're still an asshole."
"That may be so, but Rodrigo has vision. I align myself with those who have vision." Bradley started walking to Sam, and Sam responded by closing the gap on his end. The two soon stood ten feet from another as Bradley continued, "Well, I know what you're here for, and I'm happy to oblige you. I think we're due for a rematch."
Sam nodded and took the ready stance that Hanska taught him. Bradley rushed forward to attack and threw a punch. Sam swatted the blow aside while dodging and answered with one of his own. Bradley, his own senses kicking in, dodged the counter. The two began a dance of violence, both throwing a volley of blows, each one being dodged, blocked or countered.
Sam stepped in and delivered two quick jabs which Bradley ducked under. He kept bobbing his head up and down, avoiding

each strike. Sam, catching on to the pattern faked a left jab that
sent Bradley dodging downwards. On the way down, a right knee
caught him in the chin and sent him staggering back.

Sam pressed forward, kicking at Bradley as he shuffled back, trying to regain his balance. Sam moved in and narrowly dodged a punch before returning fire with two of his own. Bradley ate one of the two and covered up while Sam pressed on. Bradley caught one of his blows, slid in and headbutted Sam on the nose, drawing blood and tears to his eyes. Sam, feeling the wave of anger, came back in full force, growled and quickened the speed of his blows. Bradley was now scrambling to barely avoid contact as he caught sight of a faint glowing blue outline around Sam. The sight distracted him long enough to take a straight right to the jaw and a kick to the liver, immediately dropping him.

Bradley was struggling to catch his breath; the wind and senses were being knocked from him as Sam beckoned down at him to get up. Sam growled to Bradley, "You're not going to be a danger to anyone ever again once I'm finished here." Bradley felt a wave of panic start to come over him, seeing Sam had grown from a nervous, timid being to someone different now. Bradley decided it was time to pull the stops out, or Sam would make good on his words. Reaching deep inside, he shifted into his leopard.

Sam, seeing that Bradley was ready to go all in, shifted into his form as well and the two circled each other. Sam, being the darker hued cat, pounced at Bradley, who was a much lighter shade of orange. The two swatted claws at one another and each took a few slashes in various parts of their bodies. Bradley leapt towards Sam, who got low and heaved his body up into Bradley's ribs, driving the wind from him. Bradley crashed to the ground, awkwardly steadying himself before the impact and breaking his fall with his feet poorly.

Sam darted to Bradley, cutting around to his flank before jumping up and landing on his back. He roared and dug his claws into Bradley's haunches, getting a howl of pain from him as he began biting around the scruff of his neck. Taking him back to the ground, Sam then found the tender side of his neck and bit down, eliciting a yelp of agony from Bradley. The coppery taste of warm blood reached Sam's tongue, as he used his back claws to begin kicking and raking at Bradley's hindquarters, wounding him. Bradley attempted to get up and felt his efforts diminishing from blood loss. Fearing for his life, he roared and tried to headbutt back. Sam released his grip and swatted Bradley's head with a barrage of swipes, digging in with one claw and slamming his head into the ground. Sam then got up and crouched down near Bradley, waiting for him to move.

Bradley turned back into his human form, no longer able to sustain the leopard form as he rolled about in agony. His neck, face and legs were all bleeding as Sam shifted back into his human form. Wiping some blood off his lip, he looked down at Bradley and said, "Is that all you got?"

Looking ahead, something near Bradley's chair glowed and Sam began heading for it, while keeping his eye on Bradley. Bradley was heavily injured and could hardly move, dazed from the beating and blood loss. Sam looked down at the item to inspect it as Hanska appeared and cried, "That's the Oro Luna! Quickly! Take it and use it to seal Bradley's essence!" Sam grabbed it without a second thought and went ahead to do just that. Bradley struggled to get back to his feet and looked up to see Sam holding the seal. It began to glow yellow as Hanska said, "Hold it out, focus on the other user's essence, then draw it in. Sam did just that as he felt the tug of Bradley's essence fight against the seal. Soon, an orange transparent figure of a person was drawn out of Bradley's body and sucked into the talisman.

Bradley felt a connection sever from his body and dropped to the floor again, exhausted and weary. Sam pocketed the talisman, which was now glowing green from having sealed away an essence. He knelt down beside Bradley, saying, "Hey, you're not going to die. We're going to leave this place and I'll take you from here." Breathing heavily, Bradley responded, "Just kill me. I've failed Rodrigo, I have no more power, I'm done."

"No," Sam said as he helped a wounded Bradley to his feet. "You're either leaving with me or I'm going to take you out, by force if need be." The two slowly started leaving the atrium, and made their way through the passageways that eventually led to the exit. Squeezing through the boulders, the two got out and started heading down the mountain.

Chapter 21: Amends

It was nearly sunup when the two made it down the mountain. Sam had to help Bradley most of the way, and carried him the last bit when he couldn't walk anymore. Making his way to the car, he helped Bradley in first, then got in himself and started the car. Pulling out, he got on the road that would take them back to Keystone. Bradley was breathing hard; other than that, nothing but silence hung in the air between the two for a time. Finally, Bradley said, "You know, what's to stop me from going after you now?"

"Your condition, your resolve is crushed and my reflexes," Sam said. Bradley chuckled a bit and sat back, feeling his wounds. The blood had stopped and dried, leaving him tired and dehydrated from fighting.

"Sam...why did you not kill me? When you bit me, I thought I was done for sure."

"I wasn't going to kill you," Sam replied, sighing. "I didn't want to do that. I simply wanted to beat some sense into you."

"Well, you succeeded on that."

"You came after Fred first. That wasn't cool. Coming after Sara and myself, that was icing on the cake. I knew you were with that Rodrigo guy, and had it explained to me by the essence I have, that you were likely being manipulated."

"You can talk to your essence?" Bradley asked, bewildered.

"I can. It takes focus and meditation at first, but gets easier with time. Mine apparently is the only one that can manifest fully, being the iron shaman."

"Rodrigo was right, then. I didn't take enough time to learn the essence fully." Sam looked to Bradley and said, "What do you mean?"

"I mean he told me those very things. He said to make sure the spiritual and mental side was handled, and all I did was train on the trails."

Sam shook his head and replied, "That'll do it." Bradley laughed, coughed, then said, "You know Sam, you're a good dude. If I were in your shoes, I would've killed me for the stuff I did."

"I wanted to, make no doubt about that. But taking your life wouldn't have exactly helped when I could just stop you. I mean sure, you'd be dead, no more threat of you trying to pull any funny business, all of that. How would I explain that in person, though? A former college student got powers and attacked us in a leopard form, so I had to kill him?"

Bradley nodded and said, "It does sound ridiculous when you put it like that." Looking ahead on the road, he sat in a pool of his own thoughts. Sam felt his rage finally dissipate from him. Instead, the understanding, patient and forgiving side of his nature kicked in, the one he was always known for.

"You going to be okay, Bradley?"

"Yeah." Bradley sighed, then his tone grew heavy as he said, "I'm sorry. All of this could've been avoided had I not listened to the guy in the robes that promised me power and such. I felt...betrayed and angry when you came around. Everyone just liked you. Including Sara. I felt like you took her away from me."

"She wasn't with you to begin with. You can't make someone feel things for you. All you can do is live your life. Same thing with Sigma Pi boys. You took them for granted." Bradley softly replied, "I did, you're right. I shouldn't have."

Another moment of silence passed before Bradley said to Sam, "You think my prison sentence will be long?"

"I don't think you'll get prison. Maybe jail time, but not prison." Bradley looked back on when he first arrived at Keystone three years ago, how much fun it was, all the people he met, the fraternity: it was all flashing before him. A tear rolled down his face as he said, "Sam, please take me to the station first. I can't face the others like this."

Sam felt the remorse in Bradley and replied, "I'll visit. Maybe the others will too. That much I can do for you. I know deep down, you're not truly a bad guy. But you needed your ass kicked. Hard." Bradley laughed at Sam's humour, as Sam smiled, feeling the levity in the car grow.

A couple of hours later, once Sam dropped off Bradley at the police station and took him in himself, he drove to the Sigma Pi house and parked. Seeing one of the windows busted in, he immediately felt panic rise within, as he got out and ran inside the house. Donte and Steve were having a few beers, laughing and joking with some of the other members, with Fred and Sara now having joined them. As he walked inside, the others all shouted and greeted him.

"Is everyone okay?" Sam asked, as Sara wrapped her arms around him. Fred said to him, "There was a bit of fighting here from what the guys told me. Sara was safe with Hailey and I. We hit the road and stayed out of town for the night, just like you said." A blond-haired woman came from the kitchen and smiled at Sam.

"Oh, hello!" Sam said to her, a confused smile on his face. She replied back, "Hi! I'm Hailey. I've been seeing Fred for a few months, we kind of made things official the other day. Don't mind me!" Sam looked to Fred and said, "Ah, so this is the girl you've been seeing!"

"Yep, that's her!"

Sam looked to Donte and high fived him as he said, "How did everything go here?" Donte sighed and replied, "Bro, it's been a hell of a night. Half of the Sigma Pi guys are in the hospital. They're okay, just needed to stay overnight for their injuries. Anyways, Rodrigo came busting

hell of a night. Half of the Sigma Pi guys are in the hospital. They're okay, just needed to stay overnight for their injuries. Anyways, Rodrigo came busting up in here thinking he ran the place, right? Cut the damn power, gets Steve in full cowboy mode, and then him and I just start straight slugging it out. Big ol' cat didn't want any of this business eating these fists! Steve licked a round off in him, but the damn bastard got away. Anyways, what happened up on the mountain?"

"Bradley is at the police station, likely going to jail. He turned himself in. I got us off the mountain, he did the rest once we got there. He certainly feels bad about everything and wants me to apologize for him to you."

"Hell no! If he wants to apologize, we can all go see him and make him do it there. Sam, you don't have to do jack for him. You've done enough."

Sam laughed and replied, "So, how long until the power comes on?"

"Electric company is coming out to replace the cable later today." Sara said to the group, "Well, why don't you guys all get some shut eye and we'll go to SRV's later? I think we all could use some relaxation after this ordeal."

"Sounds like a plan!" Donte said. Sara took Sam's hand and said, "You, come with me. We're going to relax at my place. You look exhausted." As they headed out, Donte said with a grin on his face, "You said relaxation, not keeping him up any longer!" The others laughed as Sara blushed and said, "Oh shut up, you ass! Maybe I feel like keeping him up a little bit longer before he sleeps!" The entire house all exploded in laughter and cheers as the two made their way to Sara's vehicle.

Chapter 22: An Evening of Rest

Sara leaned into Sam's arms as the two laid in her bed, relaxed. Sam looked at her and said, "I'm glad you're okay." Sara shook her head and replied, "No, I'm glad that *you're* okay. I was so worried the whole night while we were gone."

"Well, at least one got to relax."

"How did everything go up there?"

"I gave Bradley the beating he needed. Thinking back to all the times he tried to hurt you or Fred, sent me over the edge."

"I'm happy you made it out okay." Sara looked at the claw mark on his arm from earlier, then a series of smaller scratches on his back. "Looks like another cat got you up here." Sam chuckled and replied, "It wasn't Bradley. Must've been some wild red-haired cat." Sara giggled and replied, "Oh my. You're just dealing with cats one after the other, aren't you?"

Sam replied, "I don't think I'll get tired of tussling with the red-headed one. She's pretty nice." Sara added, "I think she likes you too." Sam looked up at the ceiling and said, "The thing that worries me now is that Rodrigo is still out there. If he's moving freely, he may show up again with more numbers next time."

"It's a scary thought, but honestly, I wouldn't worry about him right now."

"I'm trying not to, but he's dangerous. He nearly took down all of the Sigma Pi. That's not a comforting thought."

"Well, think of it like this. You took down the only other ally that we know he had with him. That just leaves him. And I doubt he's going to come after you with all these numbers. Yes, he's a leopard, but you have the ability as well."

Sam smiled and sighed, then said, "You're right. I think a bit of rest would be good for all of us. Speaking of, I'm ready to pass out."

"Then why don't we sleep and then meet up with everyone else at SRV Steakhouse tonight, sounds good?"

"It does. It's even better with you."

By evening, everyone at the house earlier was at SRV, enjoying a grand dinner with one another. Hailey sat next to Fred, Sara with Sam, and explained the story of how herself and Fred got together.

"So, Fred then tried to out drink me in a contest of shots, and needless to say, it did not go well for him," Hailey joked as Sam laughed. Looking to his friend, he said, "Outdrank? You?! What is this world coming to?" Fred shook his head with a sheepish grin and replied, "To be fair, I had pre-gamed with the others that night before she came along."

"What led you to actually talking after that?" Sara interjected. Hailey looked at her and replied, "He's pretty cute when he's lying there quiet. He recovers nicely too. One trip to the bathroom for twenty minutes, and the next thing I know it's like he sobered up a bit. Good fortitude is fairly attractive."

At the other side of the table, Donte looked to Sam after swallowing a bite of his wings and said, "Bro, you truly have become a force of nature. I'm glad you're part of Sigma Pi."

Sam sheepishly grinned and replied, "Aw, well thanks! I'm glad to be part of the fraternity. You all are solid friends."

Steve said to him, "Next time we go hunting again, I'm bringing you, no questions. I'm ready to drop another elk and make some tasty venison."

Sara looked to Sam and asked, "Well, summer will be here soon, which means end of semester until next year. What do you plan to do?"

Sam replied, "I'll probably go visit family in Florida for the first month. Perhaps I should bring you along and have you meet them. Afterwards, maybe go sightsee the country a bit?"

Sara smiled and said, "I'd be happy to join you for all of that, if you'd have me."

Later after dinner, Sam went to his cabin to gather some of his things to stay with Sara at her place. He gathered up an overnight bag and sighed, relieved that all had returned to some sense of normalcy again.

As he walked out the door, a man in a colourful suit was standing outside of his cabin. Sam, startled at how he got there, felt his gut tighten up and asked, "Hey...can I help you?"

The man replied, "Don't mind me, Mr. Cruz. Just here to give you a proposition."

Sam looked at him for a moment before uneasily replying, "Uh...sure. Who are you?"

The man chuckled and replied, "Oh, forgive me. Where are my manners? Call me Mr. Viejas."

Sam couldn't shake the feeling that he somehow knew the man but couldn't put his finger on it as he said, "I see. Well then, what's

your proposition? Not exactly the best way to approach someone,
standing outside of their dorm waiting for them."
"I can see your cause for concern, not the best way indeed, forgive
me. Anyways, let me get to the point."

"Please do, Mr. Viejas."

"It has been brought to my attention that you possess...abilities of a special kind."

"What kind of abilities?"

"Abilities to commune with nature. To become nature. An apex predator of the jungle, as well as heightened senses. Communing with the spirit world"

Sam was now on edge, suspecting that Mr. Viejas knew of his shapeshifting abilities. Composing himself, he replied, "I'm not sure what you mean."

Mr. Viejas, his voice calm, composed, and even friendly, replied, "Oh ho, I think you do. You see, I work for a man that seeks those like you."

Sam immediately shot back, "Are you with Rodrigo?"

Mr. Viejas held up his hands, smiled under his wide brimmed fedora and replied, "Whoa, no need for such alarm! You guess correctly, Mr. Cruz. I was sent by Rodrigo to come speak to you."

"That's the asshole that sent Bradley after everyone! You have ten seconds to leave before I personally make you leave," Sam growled, his gut instinct confirmed and quickly gave way to hostility.

"He simply sent me here to ask you to join his ranks. Why not join his side, truly learn your abilities fully and become even stronger? You could stand to learn a lot from him. He is a well-lived, well-learned man that has seen and done much. You could become great under his tutelage."

"Yeah, I appreciate the offer, but I'll pass. He tried to manipulate one of our acquaintances into killing. I don't care for people like that."

"Understandable. It wasn't very becoming of Bradley to act as such. Rodrigo is a more patient, understanding man. He simply seeks to have others like you at his side."

Sam, knowing that Hanska had already explained the history of Rodrigo to him, as well as what he was truly about, was not having any of what Mr. Viejas was offering. Still, he took care to not reveal just how much he knew, and decided to play down his indignation at Rodrigo.

"That's all very tempting, Mr. Viejas, but I will politely decline. I'm quite fine with my friends and without the likes of Rodrigo. I hope he finds what he seeks in his endeavours. Just tell him to stay clear of me."

"Very well, Mr. Cruz. I see there is no swaying you. May your evening be wonderful and peaceful," Mr. Viejas replied before walking off into the night.

Sam shook his head, as he watched the suited man leave, then double checked the locks on his dorm before heading to his vehicle to drive to Sara's house.

Chapter 23: Until the Next Season

Mr. Viejas arrived at the hideout where Rodrigo was sitting with a glass of wine. Seeing the suited man return, he stood up and said, "Ah, Mr. Viejas, welcome back. Tell me, how did the offer go?"
Mr. Viejas took off his hat, revealing short black hair as he replied, "Well, he certainly refused. I don't know what you did, but he's got quite the temper towards you. Do you think he'll be a problem down the line?"
"I don't suspect he will. At least, not at first. For now, it's better to keep an eye on him and let us both coexist here peacefully. I don't intend on making this place my final home, for in my travels across the world, I've found far more intriguing places, as well as one of the shifters."
Mr. Viejas gave a quick bow and replied, "Well, I'm glad that you indeed found me, Rodrigo! I must say, this ability is simply something else. Now then, do you have leads on the others?"
Rodrigo scowled and said, "I sadly do not. Bradley lost the Oro Luna from what he told me after I visited him in jail. Said when he was battling on the mountain with Sam, it ended up falling over the side and getting lost somewhere below. I haven't found it yet, which gives me alarm for having lost it."
Mr. Viejas sighed and replied, "That is most unfortunate. Is there any other way to locate the others?"
"I can locate them through deep meditation. If one trains well enough, an essence user can detect another essence user through meditation. It's not as accurate as the Oro Luna, but it will certainly help, regardless. I've found one in Canada, off in Vancouver. That will be our next stop."
"Only two more users to find then. This will be an interesting trip. Say now, you don't suppose we could stop by a few casinos along the way, could we?"
"We could. Why, though?" Rodrigo asked, confused.
"I am an entertainer and lover of Blackjack, first and foremost. I do like hitting casinos and winning money. With this new essence and the ability to split from my body, I would like to take some casinos for their money," Mr. Viejas replied, as a transparent soul split from his body, in his image.
Rodrigo sighed and replied, "I suppose so. I'm not one for gambling, but if you say you can earn some money on it, then why not?"

Sam and Sara were having breakfast with her grandfather as Ed said to Sam, "I'm glad you whooped that dude's ass! What a tale! And I know I laugh about it now, but it also proves the legend is real. Which means that saving all the family's historical stuff on it was worth it."

Sara nodded and replied, "Grandpa, you were right about many things with this. If these things truly exist, what can we do to help? Didn't our family help them out back in the day?"

Ed took a sip from his coffee mug and said, "Well, I can start by letting you read over the stuff I've had for so long. I know your dad don't like it, but we're past that point now. I'm right, he's not, even if he's your dad."

"That's good. Do you remember your grandpa Edis?"

"He was an interesting man, that's for sure. But he was intelligent, kind and loved his family. His work was something he certainly prided himself on, but having a family helped balance it out. Grandpa Edis did make mention that wyverns used to exist. You know, dragons."

"I saw the site on the mountain. That was certainly a bone belonging to an animal that was winged and massive," Sam added.

"There you go. Now, Grandpa Edis said in his time, they were nearly hunted to extinction, but said some of the race still survived. If these shapeshifters and their powers are real, then there's a chance that wyverns may still exist in the world too. How many are left is up for debate, for they were struggling enough with their population as it were."

"Man, to think dragons are actually real. As if the shapeshifting wasn't real enough," Sam added.

Sara said, "Where did the wyverns like to live?"

Ed replied, "Mostly in mountains. They liked being away from people and places that weren't in high areas. Wyverns liked being up near the skies, where they had dominion, in a place people couldn't contest them for."

Sam took a bite of his eggs and gulped them down before saying, "I've got a feeling we haven't seen the last of Rodrigo and this shifting business."

"What makes you say that?" Sara asked.

Sam, looking pensive, replied, "Before I headed over here, there was a man that stopped by my dorm. He was offering me the chance to join Rodrigo in finding the other shifters. He was polite and friendly; I'll give him that. But if Rodrigo is recruiting others, what can that mean for us all down the line? What if he finds more to send after any of us?"

Ed explained, "The books went into detail a bit on what kind of man Rodrigo was. How he may still be. The bastard liked the idea of having his hands in the affairs of the world. That's why the Jan Damis was formed. A whole secret society of shifters across the world, placed in various locations to help influence critical key people and events. Rodrigo wanted to almost run the world from behind the scenes, from a place of anonymity."

"So, we can safely assume he is far from done on wanting to do that again?" Sam asked.

"I wouldn't assume fully, but it's likely he could aim to do something like that again. Those who taste power and lose usually want to find a way to regain it."

Sam nodded and said, "Well, if he tries anything again, I'll be ready for him. I don't care for the guy as things stand, all he needs to do is give me a reason to bury him and I will."

Ed laughed and replied, "I like the spirit, Sam! But let's not jump into anything too rashly. After all, Rodrigo isn't dumb. He's very cunning and wise to things, centuries of being alive affording him the extra experience and knowledge. Don't write him off as being so one-dimensional now. For now, it's best to let him be and just maintain an air of caution. If he's sending guys to offer you a spot in his ranks, he must feel safe enough that you yourself are no threat to him. Better you remain that way until you must actually become one."

"You're right, Ed. Better we stay our hand now and simply keep an eye on him accordingly. I'm just worried for all of us. I don't want anything to happen to any of you, especially if Rodrigo is after me."

"It's a kind notion, son. I certainly understand where you come from. If I were forty years younger, I'd go and whip his ass myself!" Sam and Sara laughed, then went on enjoying their breakfast with Ed. For now, all was right in the world.

Epilogue: A Proposal She Can't Refuse

A week later in Canada, Mr. Viejas and Rodrigo both made their way into a town in Vancouver B.C., not too far from the Washington-Canada border. The two made their way into a local bar, where a woman was sitting down at a table enjoying a plate of poutine. She had long blond hair and dark skin, and her hazel eyes sparkled with life. Her build was sturdy and robust, her curves accentuated in all the ideal places.

Rodrigo felt the familiar sense of another essence from her as he said to Mr. Viejas, "This is her. Let us greet her. Now, are you sure your idea will work?"

"Rodrigo, approaching her with the premise of power alone and dropping the mystical stuff immediately will send her running. Treat it like a business opportunity," Mr. Viejas replied. "Instead, give her the opportunity to work alongside us, give her something to gain, show how we can add value. From there, that's when you gradually drop things along those lines of the essence and show her. But people are delicate. Swaying is often best from a place of simplicity in approach."

Rodrigo nodded and said, "Very well. I'll let you take the lead. You seem to be great with people, far more than I."

Mr. Viejas nodded and replied, "We're going to need to update your wardrobe at some point as well. Looking like an extra off the set of an Indiana Jones movie isn't exactly helping you out."

Rodrigo replied with an air of offense in his tone, "These are the ceremonial tribe leader's robes. Why in the world would I replace such a grand outfit?"

"Well, for starters, you longer have a tribe. No one is going to look at you and revere you. In this time, people are going to look at you like you're nuts. We need to update your wardrobe after we leave this place."

Rodrigo sighed and said, "Fine. I bet that woman will think otherwise. Let us approach her." Mr. Viejas shook his head and replied, "I know for a fact she's going to say something about it."

The two approached her table as the woman said to them, "Hello, may I help you?"

"Greetings, madam. My name is Mr. Viejas. I operate with Leo Consulting, and I'd like to approach you with an opportunity to work with us."

"Work? I don't even know you," the woman replied apprehensively.

Mr. Viejas, eyeing a keychain that had the logo of a place called 'Burbanks Park' on her keys, said, "I do. That one visit you took to Burbanks Park left quite the impression of your talents."
The woman's eyes perked up as she said, "Oh, you mean the beer festival that recently happened there?"

Mr. Viejas, not missing a beat, replied, "The very one! We all know that LaBatt's is the golden standard here, but some of the lesser known ones there were very delicious. I like the stout from this one company...I don't remember their name though..."
"Is it a cherry tree with a maple leaf in the back?" the woman asked, her intrigue piqued by Mr. Viejas.
"I believe so. Real rich taste, notes of nuts and coffee I believe?"
"Talman's Imperial Stout!"
"That's the one!" Mr. Viejas replied, reciprocating her growing smile.
"Those are delicious!" the woman said, her affinity for beer very apparent by now.
"I am rather fond of those. The festival was a terrific time! I apologize for such an abrupt approach, didn't mean to scare you. Would you mind if my partner and I had a seat here next to you, perhaps we could get us a round of beers?"
"I would like that very much, please do!" the woman kindly replied, in much better spirits. Rodrigo and Mr. Viejas sat down in kind as the suited man called for the waitress and asked for three stouts of the same kind, the same that he said he had before.
As the waitress brought them each a beer, Mr. Viejas offered his hand behind his smile and asked, "Forgive me, what is your name, madam?"
"I'm Fiona Marois, a pleasure to meet you!" the woman replied.
"Ah, what a lovely name to go with a lovely face! My mother's name was Fiona. We've got so much in common already!" Mr. Viejas said, taking a swig of his stout.
Rodrigo was impressed by that point. Here, this man had never met this woman before, knew nothing about her, and completely bluffed his way with charisma alone. No, not charisma alone, it was more than that, but for once, Rodrigo couldn't put his finger on it. He had made the right choice in finding this man, another essence user to bring into the fold. And what a find! He had a way with people that Rodrigo could only to hope to have, compared to his days as a tribe leader.
Rodrigo wanted to know more about Mr. Viejas now, seeing him as the enigmatic man of mystery and business who seemed perfectly mercurial and, in his element, no matter where he went.
Fiona looked to Rodrigo and said, "Hi, you are?"
"Rodrigo, my dear. I work with Mr. Viejas in his consulting firm," Rodrigo replied, shaking hands with her.
Fiona giggled and replied, "I see you have an eclectic choice in clothes.

Rodrigo smiled, hiding his embarrassment and frustration that Mr. Viejas had accurately predicted she would lambast his outfit. Yet, he could only be so mad, for the man knew modern culture far better than he did, and Rodrigo knew he was going to have to adapt to the times.

Mr. Viejas, chuckling a bit, interjected and said, "He just returned from a trip from South America, forgive him. He's paying homage to the local cultures of his ancestry."

Fiona replied, "Oh wow, that's incredible! How is it down there? Where did you go?"

Rodrigo, smiling at the save and redirection Mr. Viejas set him with, replied, "Peru. I have lineage that dates back all the way to the ancient tribes that lived there. It's beautiful there. We have some business ties in Peru and will likely end up traveling there again."

Fiona, her eyes growing even wider, said, "How often do you travel?"

Mr. Viejas replied, "Quite often. Our work involves lots of travel, local research and seeing new places."

Fiona said, "Well, if I wasn't completely sold on the work before, I'm heavily interested in what you have to offer, especially if there's as much travel as you say."

Mr. Viejas smiled and replied, "Well, here's the skinny of it. Leo Consulting is a traveling consulting firm where we travel to different places and, well... consult with clients that request our services."

"What fields do you consult in?"

"Financial, real estate, contracting, and even holistic."

"I see, that's very interesting. What do you pay?"

"We work on commission. We have field agents that go to the places we send them to work as relation builders, and to get clients set up so we can close deals."

Fiona nodded her head and said, "Well, certainly beats interning up here from the sound of it. What do I have to do to sign up?"

"I have applications you can fill, which at this point would be a formality, since we approached you anyways. If you decide to take up the work, we'll start you with a thousand-dollar sign on bonus right away."

"Are you serious? You're bluffing!" Fiona cried.

Mr. Viejas reached into his jacket pocket and pulled out a stack of dollar bills, grouped in hundred bills, and spread them for her to count.

"I do not bluff with work, only when it comes to Poker," Mr. Viejas replied. "If you decline, we certainly understand and thank you for your time, considering it does involve a lot of travel."

Fiona stopped him there and replied, "Oh no, I'm in. I'll start signing on right here." Mr. Viejas handed her a pen to start signing the work as Mr. Viejas said to Rodrigo, "Why don't we give Ms. Marois some time to herself to read over everything while she fills it out?"

The two walked away from the table and went outside to speak, as Rodrigo said, "You are a being on a different level entirely, Mr. Viejas. Even I am not that convincing. Is this consultation company real though?"

"Rodrigo, it's all real," Mr. Viejas replied, pulling out business cards. "I had these made in Vegas when we stopped there to make some money. The pot I had let me open a company the next day big enough to operate small and work big. She will indeed be a legitimate employee for us."

Rodrigo smiled and looked to the sky, taking in the fresh Canadian air. He liked his new partner and their fellow companion coming on. The successor of the Jan Damis was coming, and he was excited for it.

9 781952 767005